EBURY PRESS
TO YOU, WITH LOVE

Shravya loves to keep an eye out for stories she feels are hidden all around her and then write them down. Formerly a corporate employee, she managed to flee the corporate madness after a few years of boredom, to become a full-time writer. She is a sucker for romance and strives to pen down exciting stories. When she is not reading and writing, she is out enjoying nature, playing with her dogs or cooking for her family.

She lives in Melbourne with her family, in a house with a barren backyard and a lifetime's collection of books.

She is the bestselling author of *Something I Never Told You*.

to *you,* with *love*

SHRAVYA BHINDER

EBURY
PRESS

An imprint of Penguin Random House

EBURY PRESS

USA | Canada | UK | Ireland | Australia
New Zealand | India | South Africa | China

Ebury Press is part of the Penguin Random House group of companies
whose addresses can be found at global.penguinrandomhouse.com

Published by Penguin Random House India Pvt. Ltd
7th Floor, Infinity Tower C, DLF Cyber City,
Gurgaon 122 002, Haryana, India

Penguin
Random House
India

First published in Ebury Press by Penguin Random House India 2020

10 9 8 7 6 5 4 3 2 1

This is a work of fiction. Names, characters, places and incidents are either the
product of the author's imagination or are used fictitiously and any resemblance
to any actual person, living or dead, events or locales is entirely coincidental.

ISBN 9780143450207

Typeset in Bembo by Manipal Technologies Limited, Manipal
Printed at Thomson Press India Ltd, New Delhi

www.penguin.co.in

PROLOGUE

'If I ask you to describe her in one word . . . just one word, what will that be?' she asked, looking straight into my eyes.

I could sense the excitement and eagerness in her eyes. She clearly wanted to know all that she could, just like everyone else I knew. I knew that she wanted her questions answered quickly and to her satisfaction. How did I know this? Well, she wasn't the first person whom I had met that night who wished to talk to me—almost everyone did.

I was very well aware of their intentions—the reason why, all of a sudden, my friends and their girlfriends wanted to know everything about her. Who doesn't want to talk about their beloved? Who doesn't want to brag about all their good qualities? I did too, but this sudden interest in her saddened me. It pained me to talk about her. What was I doing there that night? I should have been with her. I wanted to be with her much more than I wanted to be sitting alone at the party, staring at the stars from the terrace of Bhanu's—one of my best friends—

new house, and looking at my phone every five minutes to check the time.

'In one word! You're kidding me, right?' I asked absentmindedly, while rubbing my chin and raising my eyebrows as I pretended to ponder over her question. I was far from answering that question. My mind had drifted off in no time, and mentally, I was back with her. I wondered what she must be doing at that hour. She was all alone in the house after so long. I looked at my watch once again—it was ten at night, so she must be asleep by now, hopefully. With that thought, I came back to the present moment and decided to respond to the query of the girl sitting right in front of me. I didn't know much about this girl except for the fact that she had also been in a car accident a few years ago and was in a coma for a really long time. She was Bhanu's colleague, and Rahul's wife. Then, she had beaten cancer a few months ago and the couple was now expecting their first child. Bhanu had told me their inspiring story a million times as he begged me to keep my faith in God and miracles as this girl standing right next to me was a prime example of it.

'What is that one word that can describe her best?' I rephrased her question and concentrated hard, trying to summarize her in my head. How could I, though? She cannot be described in a single word or even a few! There were a million things about her that made her.

'Okay, try a sentence then,' she said, looking at my hands as I rubbed them together nervously and checked my watch one more time. 'I don't know, I never gave it a thought because I didn't have to describe her ever to anyone, not even to myself,' I told her absentmindedly, and took an abrupt leave from my host and his partner. They understood my situation well, and they let me excuse myself with a pat on my back and a promise that I would visit them again very soon. Both Bhanu and Pathak looked at me with pitying eyes and for some reason, I didn't mind it. For the past few months, I had seen so much pity in everyone's eyes for me that I had kind of become used to the look and it had stopped bothering me all together, unlike the way it did initially. In any case, even though I did not want their pity or sympathy, I could do nothing about how they felt for me. I did not want their company at this stage either—all I wanted and needed were everyone's prayers, and a miracle! How hard could that be!

I rushed out of the building, hailed a cab and impatiently played with my mobile as the cab drove me back home. I could not help but continuously think of that question—should I have been able to describe her? Why was this stupid question stuck in my head? I felt my mind go silent as I began thinking—so silent that I could hear the blood rush through my body. No! It is impossible for anyone else or me to sum her up in a word or even a sentence.

The girl that I am madly and hopelessly in love with is twenty-five years old. She is more beautiful than anyone else I know. She isn't perfect like a film star or the models on the cover of a fashion magazine. She has her flaws and yet she is the most beautiful person to me, because she is like art—she makes me feel alive whenever I look at her. When she walks into a room full of people, everyone looks at her because her smile is brighter than any star. She is the most positive and kindest soul I have come across, even though she has a past which is darker than the darkest nights, full of demons and stuff that nightmares are made of. Even then, she loves talking fondly about her ambitions, dreams, and passions while gazing up at the sky on starry nights—something that we have not been able to do together since quite a while; something that we need to do soon, very soon . . .

She unapologetically believes in love, luck, vibrations of souls, and destiny. She has a laugh that can make hearts melt, and her anger generally tends to fizzle out within seconds. She loves the rain and the sun equally. She is my sunshine; my warm cup of tea in the rain. Every time we cross the road together, she invariably holds on to my right sleeve—not the arm, but just the sleeve. In crowded spaces, she likes to speak to me in whispers and giggles, and each time I get irritated because I can barely understand what she is saying. The girl that I am madly and crazily in love with can look inside me, and know exactly what I want without me saying much. She knows me better and deeper than I know myself, and every time I see her, I have the same fluttering sensation in my stomach, which I first experienced when I saw her years ago. She made me understand what true love is. She has taught me that our ability to love a person not just for who they are but who they can become when loved is what makes a difference. She makes me a better person every day.

The girl I love is everything that I ever want and needed in my life.

The girl I love is dying.

I cannot forget to add here that she keeps writing these stupid notes for me that make me feel worse for not being able to do anything for her. Here in my pocket, I have the one that I found as I was stepping out to meet my friends. I had agreed to come out today only on her insistence. I do not like leaving her alone now, not even for a moment. I fear that she will be gone while I am away and if that happens, I will never be able to forgive myself.

I decided to become a writer long ago, but could never begin writing as there was no one or nothing to inspire me. But here I am, writing this book as she inspires me to follow my dreams. Here I am, writing this book only because she exists.

To You,

Again and again, I find myself on the verge of falling into countless pieces, like a shattered glass that breaks into numerous fragments that spread all over the room, waiting to be found. Sometimes, these pieces remain hidden under the surfaces, becoming witnesses to all that happens in the room. But mostly when they are discovered, they are thrown away.

I hope when I shatter because of all that is going on inside of me, bits of me stay in this room, hidden under the carpet to watch you as you live a full life, the kind that I wished to live with you, but that is a distant dream now. Life has decided our fate. Mine is to stop, but yours is to move on. It will not be easy; it will be tough, to say the least. It will be painful too but this is what I want for you. To live a life so fulfilling, and so amazing that it would bring shame to death.

Life means many things to many people and so does love—neither life nor love can be lived in a way where there is nothing new to add or nothing old to remove. Definitions change with time, place and the people who define it, yet the essence remains the same.

To me, love and life both mean you.

With Love.

This story dates back many years but let me take you to a place in time when things had just begun falling in place, the time when fate had planned for us to meet again.

Let me take you back to 2017.

CHAPTER 1

11 July 2017
New Delhi

Monsoons had not yet arrived but it was raining, and every time it rained on the scorching earth in Delhi, the smell of soil drenched in water, filled spaces and senses. I personally am not very fond of rains or was not till then. They annoyed me at times as all I could relate them to were chaotic traffic jams, water clogging, mosquitoes, power cuts . . . the list is endless. My mother used to think of me as one of the most unromantic people in the world, because only 'demons and monsters do not like rains'—her words, not mine. Both my parents are surprisingly very romantic people by the way. Being a match made in heaven, they see romance even in places where one can never imagine finding it.

But that day, things were going to change for good. I was standing at the traffic signal, waiting for the traffic lights to turn green. I was driving alone back home after meeting a friend nearby. With no desire to listen to the music on the radio, I had nothing better to do than to look around and see what other people were up to. In an auto rickshaw which was parked next to my car, was a girl. I could only see her hand. There were several mismatched bangles on her wrist. She had stuck her hand out to play with the raindrops. 'How filmy!' I muttered, being very well aware that it was not an unusual sight—many girls, as well as boys, tend to do the same sort of a thing on rainy days. And her gesture wouldn't have caught my eye had I not spotted her bright yellow dupatta hanging out of the auto. It hung very close to the rear tire—an accident waiting to happen. One thing that I have always been in my life is cautious, with a capital 'C'. Carelessness irks me more than anything else.

'What a stupid person!' I mumbled to no one in particular. The auto diver was busy on his phone and no amount of hand gestures could have made him look at me. So with no other option left, I rolled down the window in a hurry, worried as the lights went from red to orange, and pointed the dupatta to the driver. 'Bhaiya!' I called out and he looked at me with his lethargic eyes. When he gestured with his hand to ask what I was talking about, I responded by pointing towards the piece of cloth swaying in the wind. Instantly, he looked back towards his passenger and saw what I had been meaning for him to see. I rolled up my window and observed that the driver was asking his passenger to straighten up her clothing. He then lifted his hand to thank me and I smiled back at him. Unintentionally keeping an eye on the auto–rickshaw, I got lost in my thoughts when she cocked her head out in the rain to see what exactly the driver was telling her to pull back in. I saw a head full of glossy black hair starting to get wet. She moved her hair away from her face and that was when I saw her.

She still had the same eyes!

I had not seen her in years but I could still tell that it was her. She had glasses on her face, which was something new, but the rest of her was still the same. I only got a glimpse of her, so I started to roll down the window again but then suddenly my phone rang. The ringtone startled me, and clumsily, I checked the name of the caller. It was my mother. Before I could decide whether to call out her name or not, the lights turned green, and the yellow and green auto swiftly moved away from me. Soon, there were tons of people who decided to blow their horns at me as my car was not moving and people behind me were stuck.

Wondering if I was mistaken or if it was really her, I too moved into the traffic. I had lost sight of the auto-rickshaw as it must have zoomed through the traffic zig-zagging between the tiny spaces, the way all auto-rickshaws usually do.

It did look like her. I hope it was her. I resolved to trace her and find out if she was in Delhi again after so many years.

The next evening . . .

Not a lot of people were out shopping in the mall that day, which was a good thing for me as I was on a very tight schedule. I am a very opinionated person who also has a negative opinion about most things in life. For example, rain, according to me, is boring and dull, and shopping is overrated. I have never been a big fan of shopping in a mall or a market. I prefer online shopping if I have to buy anything at all. Mostly, it is my mother who likes to shop for me and I make peace with her choices.

That evening was different, as I had finally been able to get away to live on my own in Bengaluru for the last two years. Being the only child of my parents who loved pampering me at every given opportunity, this was a perfect time for me to be an adult. So as an adult, I decided to shop for my own things, with my mother's help of course! After graduation, I had taken a one year planned break to try and see if I could crack a medical entrance examination. Sadly, I couldn't. Soon the one year planned break turned into two and three, and I failed, again and again, to make it to the list. It was probably because I was not very keen on becoming a doctor as such. My professional life was charted in front of me ever since I was a teenager, and by failing the exams, all I was doing was essentially taking breaks from my studies and delaying taking up my role.

By the end of the second year, I had started investing some time every week to help my father out in his business and I knew that it gave me all the thrill that I needed in my life.

No, I am not complaining, I have had an amazing life, but one thing that I always wanted to do was to live on my own and experience life, a *real* life, with *real* problems. I wanted to do all this in the prime of my youth and probably this was why I wanted to study in a medical college too.

After two of my best mates from college, Bhanu and Ali, moved to Bengaluru some years ago, I started feeling that my father's company and I could both benefit from an MBA degree, especially if I did it from Bengaluru. So, in 2017, I finally asked him if I could study for a couple of more years. 'Just two more years, Papa,' I begged him, and my filmy dad held on to my right hand, lifted it only to let it go, stating Om Puri's famous dialogue in the blockbuster movie, *Dilwale Dulhaniya Le Jayenge*—'Ja Simran ja, jee le apni zindagi' (Go Simran, live your life). My mother rolled on the sofa laughing. Did I tell you that my father loves Hindi movies? Well, he is a big movie buff and so is my mother. I am more of a reader and writer, I would say.

So finally, I was all set to go and live on my own for two whole years. But the initial feeling of excitement somehow turned into anxiety over a month after my enrolment was confirmed. If you ask me why, my answer would be simple—because of my paranoid mother! She made me realize how I do not enjoy the process of making new friends and acquaintances by pointing out as many as million instances right from the time I was born to the present day, in the duration of which I had not made many friends. I do agree that I didn't really want to make new friends so much and if given a choice, I would rather revive an old friendship than form a new one. 'A flaw' as my father calls it, though I think of it as a boon; it keeps me loyal to those who have been around me for long. Anyhow, with my travel plans arranged by my father's secretary and two friends to keep me company in the new city, I was set to fly in a couple of days and was almost done packing. My loving mother kept on counting things after things that she felt I would need while I was away from her.

I, on the other hand, failed miserably at reminding her that I was going to a metropolitan city, which has almost everything that Delhi has to offer and more, but each time I mentioned it to her and explained that I was not going to go and live on Mars, she looked at me as if I was talking in some alien language. 'But it is a different place altogether! Your chachi (aunt) had gone to live there for a week and she couldn't find one restaurant which served decent daal makhni.'

'Urgh!' was all that I could utter. She had proved a point once again even though it was so unsuitable for a situation like this one. She was so good at convincing me that I agreed to go out shopping with her thinking that *I* was the one in charge!

So, there I was, trying clothes after clothes at a mall near our house. Finally, after what felt like an eternity, I stood with a heap of clothes in my shopping bag, in a queue at the billing counter when I heard my mother call out my name, 'Sahil!'

I turned around to look for her only to find someone else standing right behind me in the queue. She had the same dark-rimmed glasses covering half of her tiny face, and was also chewing on her fingernail. I remembered this not-so-pleasant habit of hers from the time we were in school. She looked as mousy as she did back in those days. Surprisingly, I was looking at her after years and yet it appeared as if not a lot of time had passed. Memories started hitting my overworked and semi-frozen brain one after the other. The not-very-tall, fair-skinned girl with a sharp, pointed nose and big, brown almond eyes stood right in front of me unaware of the mental journey that I had been making with her into our past.

I used to call her my 'Minnie Mouse' back then and she was the sole reason why I flunked a subject, the only time that I had, which is a different and a very long story.

Is it really her? I asked myself in disbelief and stared at her with my eyes popping out, waiting for her to get off her phone, on which she was now carelessly scrolling. My heart was pounding very fast as if someone had pressed the accelerator on it and forgotten to take their foot off. *It was indeed her!* I felt my blood rush through my body. She had a few clothes tucked under her right arm as she moved her delicate fingers up and down her phone. Honestly, she had turned a little too geeky since I'd last seen her. She had to be renamed 'Miss Geeky Minnie Mouse'! I chuckled at my small joke which was unusual of me as I hardly ever saw humour in any situation—one of my actual flaws. This also proved that it was her that I saw a day before in the auto-rickshaw. 'She loves the rains and I do not!' I said to myself.

I looked at her again, thinking whether or not I should say something to her, maybe a conversation starter: *Hi?* I was worried about being mistaken. So many years had passed, and the world is full of dopplegängers.

You cannot be mistaken about this. It is her, I thought to myself. There is no way I could have gone wrong about identifying this girl. I can, in fact, identify her even in a room full of nerds. It seems like my sense of humour was on fire that day, or maybe I was finding my jokes funny because of my semi-frozen brain cells. Suddenly, I recalled our last meeting and my hands reached up to cover my eyes. *No, no, no! You cannot talk to her,* I reminded my stupid self and covered my face, even though she had not even once moved her eyes away from her phone to look at me. Sometimes smartphones can be extremely helpful to save awkward people like me from embarrassment.

While I still had my hands over my eyes, someone poked me in the stomach. It was none other than my dear mother. I did hear her calling out my name more than a few times in the last few minutes but her voice had faded in the background as my mind worked on how to strike a conversation with the girl. My mother now stood right between the two of us, blocking my view of her. 'This is for the best,' I decided, and then concentrated on my mother so that the unnecessary banter in my head could stop.

'I think you should get this one too,' she told me, as I finally turned back to face the billing counter to avoid the situation.

'Sure,' I responded to her casually, fully aware that she must have observed my actions and reactions and would grill me with her questions later. My mother has an elephant-like memory and nothing escapes her hawk-eye vision. A deadly combo in a mother I tell you—you can seldom hide anything from her. I have been on the planet for more than twenty-six years already and am still trying to figure out a loophole in her god-gifted expertise.

I could sense my mother turn around for a glance to scan the one who had stolen all my attention from her. Knowing her well, I can tell you what must have happened: like a pro, Mummy would have looked behind her on the pretext of adjusting her handbag and then turned back to face me in a split second. Why do I not possess this skill? I should have been gifted with such stealthy moves and smart tactics! Mummy doesn't even need those. But I do, most desperately too.

'Go and try this one now,' she commanded, refocusing her attention on me. I checked the tag on the jacket; it was marked 'Medium'.

'There is no need, it will fit me just fine,' I replied, and Mummy looked at me with disapproval as I dumped the black jacket on top of the heap of clothes.

'I think you should still try it on,' Mummy insisted.

She was right. Again. The jacket did not fit me well when I finally tried it on after coming back home. My arms are a tad smaller than the usual size and most ready-made clothes like shirts and jackets do not fit me well. They are built for people with normal arms, while I have miniature ones. The sleeves are usually an inch longer than required and I get them tailored almost every time. But at that moment, I didn't want to leave the queue so I insisted that the jacket would fit me just fine.

A while later, after paying a hefty bill at the counter, I walked away with my mother, who still wanted to shop a little more. No matter how much I itched to turn around and look at that girl one more time, I did not dare to do so in my mother's presence.

I am Sahil Malhotra, the only child of Mrs and Mr Malhotra of A-170, Defence Colony, New Delhi. Unlike me, my parents have a very colourful life and I feel that they deserve the next chapter to themselves so that their story can be told in a way that it deserves to be told.

Till we reach there, let me finish telling you about that eventful day at the mall.

'Who was that girl?' my mother impatiently asked me one more time as we waited at a watch store for the attendant to bring our bill.

'Which girl?' I acted naively again, but was fully aware that nothing escaped Mummy's eyes or ears. 'The girl who was standing right behind you in the queue at Tommy Hilfiger; the one you were looking at. Is she from your college? I met her in the ladies' section and she said "Namaste Aunty." She knows me for sure.'

What? My mother got to talk to her and I didn't! I was itching to ask her if the girl said anything else too but I refrained from getting carried away. I knew that would make her interrogation worse. Anyway, I did know that she would eventually make me talk. I knew it so well, then why was I even trying? Well, even a gazelle gets to try and outrun a tiger. It can't do so but it still tries. So, I too was attempting to outrun my mommy tiger. 'Hmmm,' she gave a sigh a moment later to signal her disappointment, and then she cast her eyes on the floor like she did when she wanted her way.

An emotional round of interrogation was to begin and I wanted to avoid it at any cost. I pretended to fix my hair and avoid eye contact, but she kept her expectant gaze on me. I had to tell her who the girl was. 'She was Ayra—Ayra Sharma from my school,' I tried to remind her. She would recall her from her name and I knew that, but with my mother, one never knows what will come out of her mouth next.

I waited for her to say something as she tried to recall her name with a frown on her face, 'Ayra?' she repeated and then abruptly and very loudly added, 'The girl from your kindergarten whom you wanted to marry?'

'Ma!' I said, slapping my palm loudly on my forehead. The entire store looked at me, and to be honest, I did hear a few suppressed giggles too. 'It was not in the kindergarten, Ma!' I corrected her in whispers.

CHAPTER 2

Coming to my parents now, I think that they can make a movie about their lives and it should be titled, '1988, A (Malhotra) Love Story'.

He first saw her while she was watering plants in her balcony opposite to the flat where he was staying. In his own words, Rajesh described the moment their eyes met as the moment he felt an instant connection with her—something too powerful to be put into words. Rajesh Malhotra had been staying with his newly-wed sister and her husband in their apartment in Mumbai for the past one week. As a New Delhi boy who was a movie addict and a self-confessed, obsessed fan of Amitabh Bachchan, he wanted to meet and greet his idol, and had been pressuring his new brother-in-law to arrange a meeting. His brother-in-law, who worked at a recording studio in Mumbai, couldn't say no to Rajesh's request as Rajesh was his only brother-in-law, and someone who was dearly loved by his new bride.

After a few phone calls here and there, he informed Rajesh that unfortunately, Mr Bachchan was shooting abroad at that time and was to return only after three weeks. So, Rajesh, the son of a bank clerk was advised to return home and come back again, a month or two later. Rajesh also had to go back to Delhi and sit for the Bank PO exams. He was not very keen on living the same life that his father had lived, even when he could find no fault in it, but he had bigger dreams. He wanted to do something in his life. What exactly that 'something' was, he was yet to figure out.

Also, he was very fascinated by the world of cinema. He knew that he had neither the looks to become a hero nor the voice to become a singer—two professions that he really looked up to. So, in order to try and figure out if there was something other than those two professions which would suit him, he decided to overstay his welcome in the 'city of dreams'. No matter how much his brother-in-law disliked his prolonged stay at their home, his wife insisted that he stayed with them for as long as he liked. Rajesh took up the offer and called back home to let his family know. There was only one condition for his stay—he had to earn while he was there. So, he started accompanying his brother-in-law to his workplace every day. He did manage to get a few odd jobs every now and then, but the struggle destroyed all his Bollywood dreams.

Soon, he got bored of working on the sets and started staying back at home with his sister. She had settled in her new life and had lesser and lesser time to devote to her younger brother. With no work or friends in the new place, a lonely Rajesh passed the next few days wandering around in the building at its clubhouse, and spending the evenings at the parks inside the building. His muse from the other building too came there with her niece, so that the child could play with her friends. When he heard her talk for the first time and noticed the way her eyes lit up when she was talking about something, he knew that she was the one for him. They sat in the parks every day for hours, talking. Innocent love blossomed and intoxicated, just like in the movies *Dil* and *Aashiqui*. Rajesh asked his neighbour to accompany him to a movie a week later! This was apparently a scandalous thing to do in those days, but love is never scared of scandals, as they say.

Once she agreed to go out with him, Rajesh or 'Raj' as he was fondly addressed by her, also confessed his love for the girl in the neighbourhood to his sister. He believed that she had the right to know before anyone else did as she was the girl's local guardian in the city. He told her that he had fallen in love with the girl who reminded him of Nagma, the actress. When his sister realized that he had been talking about a wealthy, non-Hindu girl who was most probably engaged to be married to one of their acquaintances, she warned him of the consequences. But Rajesh was determined to marry Anisa Irani, his Parsi love, after falling in love with her light blue eyes.

When he cancelled his ticket to go back home—even after meeting Amitabh Bachchan—his father threatened to disown him. That was when he had to give in. Rajesh went back only to keep returning now and then, when he couldn't afford a ticket to Mumbai (then Bombay); instead, he wrote letters to her. For two years, they wrote to each other in secret after which Anisa's brother got hold of a love letter before it could be delivered to Rajesh's girl.

Anisa called Rajesh to let him know that she was being forcefully married to someone else. Borrowing a sum of five hundred rupees from a dear friend, Rajesh was in Bombay three days later. He met her parents and told them that his love for their daughter was true and he intended to marry and keep her very happy all her life, but they asked him to forget her. Her father, a rich and reputed Parsi merchant, had chosen a well-to-do boy for his only daughter. As expected, Rajesh was beaten black and blue and no one came to support him.

The same night, Anisa ran away from her house, and the love birds took the next train to Delhi. Once in Delhi, they got married. Anisa was disowned by her loving family. Rajesh became a Bank PO, and after one year, they welcomed a baby boy whom they named Sahil. Yes, that is me. I couldn't *not* have made an entry into this love story when I am the one narrating it.

When I was around ten years old, my father and one of his best friends, Pankaj Mehra—the same dear friend who had lent him the money to elope—ventured into IT outsourcing. My father left his job and took loans to support the business. For three years, my mother became the bread-earner for the family, as Papa was still establishing his business. She supported him through thick and thin and Papa rightly calls her his 'king-maker'. She not only encouraged the son of a clerk to dream big, but she also stood by his side as his dreams became a reality. She, with her knowledge of family businesses helped him work out finances and grow his assets. Today, the same business is worth many crores, and we are what the society refers to as 'new money'. We have the money but do not know where to spend it.

My parents raised me up in a middle-class environment and even today, I have to seek their permission to spend their money because it is *their* money.

My parent's mantra for life is very straightforward. They say that life is simple; we need to free ourselves from the net that society has woven around us and live it the way we want to. Only when one does so, is one truly happy. Live each moment and experience the beauty of it.

Enough of their love story; let me now take you back to mine.

CHAPTER 3

2017, New Delhi

After gawking at her in the queue at the mall and still unable to talk to her, I found myself tracing my memory to figure out how much I remember of her. The first realization for me was that my first memory of her is blurred, like a dream or a hazy evening when one is too sleepy to remember all the details. It was years ago when we first met and unlike what my mother remembers, we didn't meet during kindergarten. We met later at my school. She had just taken a transfer from a different school somewhere in the world, and walked into my life, only to disappear again later. Despite my parents' fluctuating financial status, one thing that remained constant was my school. They knew that too many changes would disrupt my childhood, so they decided against moving me into a better school even when they made money. Even during the times when they struggled with money, they made sure that my school fee was still paid on time. This is why I feel that they are the best parents in the world.

Even though my parents tried to control the number of changes that rocked my life, there were a few changes which they had no control over. It was the beginning of class four when a few students had left school and a few new ones had replaced them. That year was a little difficult for me as my grandfather, who I was really close to, had passed away. He was the one who would pick and drop me from school every day. Later, my mother took up that responsibility, but the void—emotional as well as psychological—remained despite all the praiseworthy efforts from both my parents to fill it. Also, my bench partner of that time, Shrey, had to leave school as his father who was in the police force was transferred to Ranchi. So, with two major recent losses, on the first day of the new term, I sat in the classroom at the last bench, alone, sulking and waiting for the day to be over as soon as it began.

After the first period was over, she walked in with our class teacher, Vibha ma'am. She was late for her first day and walked beside the teacher with her head bowed down. Ayra Sharma, a new student who was the exact opposite of how I was, decided to storm into my life and become my best friend. She walked straight up to my desk and asked me if she could take the seat next to mine, in a very low voice. I saw that her hands were shaking and she fluttered her eyelids too much. She looked like one of those dolls in toy shops—the ones that have pale faces and big fluttering eyes. The only difference was that this one spoke too and in a very irritatingly sweet sort of way. I wanted to tell her that she could not take the seat as it was reserved for my best friend, or something else which was going to be very complex for her tiny head, but our class teacher accompanied her so I did not give her a smart reply, which I otherwise would have. I moved my bag aside and gave her some space to fit her tiny frame in. She was shorter than most of the other kids in my class, and that was the moment I decided to name her Minnie Mouse. I, in fact, mumbled it under my breath, hoping that she would hear me and go sit somewhere else. But she didn't care about what I, or anyone else thought of her; she lived in her world and she had an annoying habit of chewing her nails as she read what was written on the blackboard.

She usually copied everything from my notebooks. For the first few days we kept our school bags between us as if they were walls. I do not remember much of what happened later on the first day or many other days when she sat next to me. What I do remember is that much to my initial dislike, the nail-biting Minnie Mouse sat next to me in class for the rest of the year. Being the cute kid that I was, I could only guess why! I forgave her for intruding into my personal space and taking over the seat which I thought belonged only to Shrey. Sometime later, we became such good pals that the wall of bags was no longer needed and Ayra and I were talking all day, every day, and being punished for sitting with our heads joined together laughing at other kids.

I do not remember exactly when in a few months the younger me realized that my new friend had two different personalities. She was a chatterbox with me and a very shy and docile girl with all the other kids as well as with the teachers. Her behaviour at times confused me and sometimes it made me proud of my friendship with her. She barely spoke with anyone other than me at school and shivered if the teacher asked her a question in front of the whole class. Her sassy answers and talkbacks were reserved for me alone and she refused to make more friends even though many kids wanted to get to know her better. Why she so was a mystery to me, but I was happy to have her all for myself and never bothered to explore deeper to understand her behaviour. Kids don't do that; they do not judge. They just love wholeheartedly, the way we did.

We ate our lunch together on most days. I told Mummy to pack lunch for her too as she often forgot to bring her lunch box, or that was what she told me. While I topped my class in almost all subjects, she fared well in a few subjects and was a below-average student overall. Our parents used to see each other at parent-teacher meetings where I was always praised, while she was mostly criticized. I once saw her mother hit her on the school grounds after the parent-teacher meeting. When I later asked her what happened, she dismissed me by saying that I was cooking up lame stories to entertain myself. I never spoke about the incident with her or anyone else ever again. I had never been struck by my parents, but I did know that many of my classmates had. It was a norm back then, so I concluded that Ayra was embarrassed about what happened, which is why she was unwilling to admit that what I saw was true. 'Not a very big deal!' I told myself and my life resumed.

From class four till eight, we sat together every day and she and I became best friends. Her family stayed in a rented house somewhere near my uncle's (my father's cousin) house, so I started visiting my uncle more frequently than I visited any other relative. Sometimes, I was able to go to Ayra's home and spend time with her. We used to call each other on our landline phones and talk about cartoons, my dogs, video games and sometimes even studies. My mother liked her a lot, but I didn't get a very positive vibe from her parents who referred to me as a 'brat' behind my back. I understand now that they must have thought that I, with the 'new money and privilege' around me was probably a bad influence on their daughter, but back then, I hated her mother and wondered how she had a daughter like Ayra. They did not even look alike.

When we reached class nine and matured a little, I wanted to know more about Ayra's parents' disapproval of me. I asked her why her mother disliked me so much, and that's when she started telling me a little more about her family members. One day, after school, she told me that she wanted to talk to me about something. I remember her stuttering a little, trying to look for words and then crying inconsolably. She told me that she felt weird around one particular cousin. I asked her why? 'Does he hit you?' was the first thing that came to my head.

'No! No, no. It is not that,' she told me sobbing, 'I just think that he is a bully. Shall I tell Mummy about him?' She asked me with wet eyes that had a lost look in them.

I was as young as she was and didn't know what to tell her. I could have told her that she should talk to her parents, or I could have probed her more to understand what it was that made her so mad at this cousin. I could have told her to confront him before his family, but I did none of those things that I now think I should have. Instead, I remember assuring her that I would fight this bully cousin of hers and he would never trouble her again, to end the uncomfortable topic as all I wanted at that point was for her to smile at me, like she always did. She did give me a weak smile a while later. When I told her once again that I was going to bash this cousin of hers she told me to shut up and both of us began jotting down our History notes—I from the blackboard and she from my notebook. That was the end of the topic as I knew it. These are the things that I clearly remember from the time when Ayra and I were studying together.

What my mother remembers is only one instance from my thirteenth birthday when I had invited Ayra. She was permitted to come over with her sister, who I recall was a snob and a party-spoiler. She loved bossing around younger kids, and Ayra followed her like a puppy. Her parents were mostly not in favour of sending their daughters anywhere new, but my mother insisted so much that Ayra's mother had no option but to agree. Our driver picked them up from their home and dropped them to our house just in time for the cake-cutting. I remember shamefully announcing that I would not cut or let anyone else cut the cake until she arrives. After she arrived, I followed her around and more than a few kids noticed it. On being teased by a cousin who called her my 'girlfriend', I told him that she was not my girlfriend and pushed him so hard that he hit the ground and began whining in pain.

As the boys engaged in a loud fight of words over her position in my life, a worried Ayra wanted to know what had happened, and who or what exactly a 'girlfriend' was. Pulling my collar out of my cousin's fist, I, as calmly as I could, explained to her that a girlfriend is someone you get married to. In my defence, this was what I was led to believe by my parents till then.

'I told him that as you and I are not getting married and you are not my girlfriend, we are just friends,' the ten-year-old me assured my female friend.

'I do not mind getting married to you,' she told me, surprising me a little as she took my hand.

My cousins laughed, but I was amazed at her and didn't bother to respond to their laughs or the snickering noises that they were making to make her nervous.

'See, let us make a pact here. If you and I do not find our girlfriends by the time we are twenty-five, we become each other's girlfriend. And we get married to each other, okay?' she said. She fluttered her eyelids and I saw a sparkle in her big brown eyes. The sparkle that made me realize that her friendship was the best thing that I had. The docile girl commanded me to agree with her.

'Okay,' I told her raising my eyebrows, 'but Ayra . . . ' I wanted to tell her something else when my mother giggled from behind us. She had heard us! She held my arm and took me away from her; it was time to cut the cake. I wanted to tell Ayra that I would be her 'boyfriend', but I never got a chance to correct her as the topic never came up after the party, partly because I was shy and majorly because the life

of pre-teens is too happening to close open discussions—
every day there was something new, and something better
to talk about.

When we graduated to class ten, Ayra turned into a
slightly different person who would have terrible mood
swings, and I always wondered what had happened. There
were days when she would not discuss anything with me
and even tell me to let her be. I was her only friend. But
that was not the case for me—I had managed to make a
few more friends in class, and a few in my tuition class, and
I wondered if that irked her. She would later come back
and apologize for her behaviour. My mother explained
to me how people change over time and that there is not
necessarily anything wrong in their lives for them to be
behaving differently. But I chose to follow what my instincts
told me. I knew that something was wrong and that she
wouldn't share it with me. I could tell that she was the same
person because her eyes never changed and yet something
had changed.

After the first two months, Ayra and her sister left our
school for a school that promised better education. She
promised to be in touch with me the day she broke the
news. I remember crying alone in the classroom and telling
a friend that I liked her a lot. She couldn't keep what she
had heard to herself and walked straight up to Ayra to tell
her that I 'liked' her more than a friend. I was sitting in the
class alone during lunch when Ayra stormed in, her eyes
red with all the crying and her face puffed up due to anger.
Without asking or hearing anything, she just called me a
'stupid brat' and walked out. I never heard from her again

as her family moved houses and my wait for a phone call from her died a natural death with passing time. I knew that I had lost a friend.

Coming back to the day after I saw her at the mall.

New Delhi, my home
5 a.m.

Finding her there in the mall made me recall almost every little detail which my mind had preserved in some sweet little corner. Our innocent friendship was precious to me and I wanted to know more about her; I wanted to know if she was still the same girl who became my friend during my worst phase; I wanted to know if she spoke the same way, laughed the same way and loved the same way. In today's day and age, it is very simple to look someone up. Go to Google and type in their name, their Facebook, Instagram, Twitter and everything else that they would have ever shared with the world on the web would be served to you on a platter. This is the case mostly, but not always. I tried all the permutations and combinations of her name, age, and location to find an active social media account.

Ayra Sharma
Ayra Sharma Gurgaon
Ayra Gurgaon
Ayra Delhi
Ayra New Delhi

I tried it all and nothing worked. We had no common friends as she maintained no connections with anyone at school. Three hours of fruitless searches later, it hit me—she had an elder sister, who was immensely popular in school. But what was her name? I tried hard to recall.

A few hours passed and I was still trying to recall her sister's name. My mind did not let me forget anything at all about the moment when Ayra had called me a 'stupid brat'. I remembered the way she looked at me, the maths equation which was written behind her on the board, and the pasta Mummy had packed for our lunch which I ate alone. But my mind conveniently forgot her sister's name! God should never punish any other human being the way he has punished me by bestowing me with what I refer to as my 'flash memory'—in a flash I can recall it all and, in a flash, all of it goes away too. So, while I was waiting for the flash to make an appearance, I managed to pack my bags for my evening flight to Bengaluru, and had a hearty breakfast with my parents who wanted me to go and have some fun before taking up the family business.

'You are no fun, my son,' my father loves rhyming his words on occasions when no rhyming was needed. In fact, I wonder if anyone other than school kids need to rhyme anything, but then I am very opinionated.

'I am *normal*, Papa. You guys are too much fun, trust me!' A smart answer was right there from his 'no-fun-son'.

He gave me a 'what do you know about us, you silly boy' smile and patted my back. 'If nothing, try and make some new friends and come back with a wife!' he joked.

I was itching to tell him that I would, if and only if my memory wouldn't fail me too often. *Was I thinking of marrying her? What if she had a boyfriend? What if she was married already? What if she had changed as a person? No, she couldn't have changed.* I zoned out on my father who snapped his fingers in front of my face to bring me back from 'planet Ayra'. 'I am on it,' I told him with a wink, hoping that the topic was over, but it was far from it. He went on to make sad jokes about how their wedding was pocket-friendly and I should follow the same course and send them pictures instead of invites to the wedding. 'Boy, I will miss them,' I told my reflection in the bathroom mirror as I heard my mother—sitting outside in the living area—giggle to another one of my father's lame jokes. They were the image of perfection in my eyes and I was an exact opposite in theirs.

That evening things were as normal as they could be in the household. I was even starting to regret my decision of going away as my parents were eagerly waiting for me to leave so that they could relive the time when it was just the two of them together. Argh—the love birds! In the afternoon, phone calls started pouring in like monsoon rains. One after the other, all long-lost relatives called my parents to know about my travel and other plans.

What time was the flight? Where shall I be staying? What course have I signed myself up for? Why was I moving to a new city? Had I been in a fight with my parents recently? Have my parents been looking for a girl for me to get married to? Did I just come out of the closet? Et cetera, et cetera.

Such phone calls are customary in a big Punjabi family like ours, and over the last many years of receiving them like clockwork before all our holidays and trips, I was a pro at ducking most of the questions in the list; yet, the relatives never tire in their attempt of digging some sort of gossip from every household to be discussed at the next family gathering, wedding or death ceremony. Life or no life, gossip is a must!

While taking the last of my customary calls, it happened—the flash finally hit my brain at lightning speed. Her sister's name was Somya Sharma. 'Yes!' I couldn't contain my excitement and screamed while talking to my *mama*, my maternal uncle, who a few years ago had finally forgiven my parents for eloping.

'What happened?' Mama asked worriedly.

'Nothing!' I told him, grinning like an idiot, trying to control my itching fingers that were ready to type the name into a search engine and finally connect with Ayra. *I think you are obsessing over her just like you used to in school*, I warned myself. It is tough to keep your thoughts in check, especially when your mind believes that it is a know-it-all.

So, fifteen minutes and three searches later, I managed to find Ayra's sister's Facebook account, which was as restricted as any girl's account can be. I managed to locate a few of her tagged images and while scrolling through them I finally found her: *Itsmeayra*. I sent her a friend request mentioning who I was, hoping that she remembered some bits of the time that we had spent in each other's company, long ago. As expected, she and I had no common friends and until she accepted my request, there was not a lot that I could access on her account; the same was the case with her Instagram. I patiently waited for her to respond, hoping that she remembered me and praying that she was single.

Three hours went by and I checked my phone every time it beeped, hoping that it was her, but it wasn't. Finally, at five in the evening, my parents, my cousin and I started our journey to the airport. It was a pleasant surprise to have encountered close to no traffic jams on our way, and soon, we reached our destination. While I was arranging my luggage on the trolley at the airport, Papa got a call from someone on his staff. He signalled Mummy, Sameer, and me to carry on towards the entry gate, while he stood at the same place to answer the call. My flight was at 6.45 pm and like always, we were at the airport before time. Sameer, who is a distant cousin and a great friend, had accompanied us to the airport. I believe that the sole purpose of his visit was to make fun of the kilos of luggage that I had packed to take along with me. 'Ha, ha, ha. Laugh as much as you want. The next time you go somewhere, I too shall weigh all your bags!' I mocked him to end the topic but he wouldn't let go. The three of us—Sameer, Mummy and I kept on looking at Papa signalling him to wrap up the call soon.

Five minutes and several hand gestures later, Papa hung up the call and walked towards us. 'What happened? Is everything okay?' Mummy asked him, looking as tensed as Papa was.

'A staff member has suffered a stroke,' he replied worriedly. He loves all his employees and takes care of them like his own family. He even wishes all of them personally on their birthday through e-mail and picks up all calls no matter what time of the day it is.

'Who?' Mummy placed a hand on his shoulder and asked. Her voice was soft but her concern couldn't be hidden.

'Sharma,' came his reply. Mr Sharma was the manager in one of the branches in Noida. He was the same age as my father; they had even studied together for a few years in college. He was a frequent visitor at our home as well. I felt sad for him as well as for my father who looked deeply saddened. 'Would you like to go and see if they need anything?' I encouraged my father to do the right thing and he nodded.

'Sameer will drop Mummy home,' I added and hugged my father. When we let go of each other, for the first time, I realized that age was taking over him too. His once firm and strong shoulders were not that strong anymore; he had wrinkles around his eyes and he wore glasses even when he was not reading. I felt a sudden ache in my heart. 'Am I doing the right thing by going off to study for two more years?' I wondered. Parents know what you are thinking even when you say nothing. My parents are no different. Sensing the trouble in my head, my father hugged me once again and said, 'Go and get this MBA done so that you can come back and help me out okay? I need a qualified manager for my business in two years' time.'

'Yes . . . okay' was all that I could manage to say to him, looking at my shoes and nodding my head. 'Was I really doing the right thing by going away?' I wondered.

After my father left, I checked the status of my flight—it was on time. I was relieved, for I hate waiting for flights, trains or buses. That was it; it was time for me to go. I nervously smiled at my mother, who looked as if all the blood had, within a fraction of a second, been sucked out of her body. I understood her concern as well as her feelings. After all, her only son was moving to a new city. 'So Ma, what will you do for the next two years?' I teased her hoping to lighten her mood and the atmosphere around us. I had expected Sameer to do this but he was too busy scrolling on his phone to remember his brotherly duties. I believed that I had managed to do a good enough job with that question, but to my surprise, the waterworks began unannounced. My mother cried her heart out and finally just before I was to go in, she said, 'Take care of yourself, for you are all I have.' A lump formed in my throat and I hugged her tightly before waving goodbye.

With a promise to call them as soon as the plane landed, I set off on my first solo journey. I was used to travelling a lot with my parents, but travelling alone was not the same. I handed over all my luggage at the check-in and collected my boarding pass. Once I got past the security check, I looked for a cafe to get some coffee. I was awake for more than twelve hours by then and the overtly emotional scene outside the airport had taken a toll on me. I decided to not access the airport lounge and took a seat at a cafe instead. One after the other, I got two messages from Sameer. Both him and Mummy had reached home safely. I called Papa to check the health of Mr Sharma. Thankfully, he was stable too. Finally, the boarding call was announced and I went into the plane.

Bright and chirpy hostesses welcomed me aboard and I fastened my seat belt. Finally, when the take-off was announced, I checked my phone once last before switching it off, for an alert from Facebook, only to be disappointed once again. My friend request was still pending. My brain was tired and so was my body; it was not going to be a long flight, but any rest was better than no rest. So, I switched off my phone, closed my eyes and thought of the advice Papa gave me a night before. His words echoed in my ears as I gave my tired eyes a much-needed time off.

'I am so glad that you are finally taking a step forward and breaking the stagnancy in your life. Sahil,' Papa had said placing his hand lovingly over my shoulders, 'Remember to focus on actions. It is not our thoughts but our actions that can end years of stagnation in one go. A step no matter how small is all that it takes. Always trust your gut. Your intuition will lead your life in the direction that it is meant to go in and you will find the purpose of your life.'

I was going to focus on actions. 'Chasing perfection takes you nowhere, but chasing progress takes you places'— this was going to be my motto for my life ahead.

CHAPTER 4

August 2017
Bengaluru, India

My parents had an apartment in Bengaluru city, which they had purchased a few years ago for investment purposes. For many years, an elderly couple had rented the place and from the looks of it, it was not wrong to say that they loved and maintained the house as their own. Three months ago, when the husband passed away and the wife moved to Canada to live with her only daughter and her family, my father decided not to put it out for rent again. My admission was confirmed by then and it only made sense that I lived in our house instead of the college campus. I intended to stay at the place for the next two years that I planned to be in the city and being the spoilt child that I was, I needed help. So, Mummy had organized a very nice and shy house help, Jagjeet, to help me out in the new city. Jagjeet was the son of my Papa's distant cousin and was almost as old as I am. I had a few phone calls with him in the last few weeks where he explained to me what was to be expected from the place. He and I had never met before in our lives. From my mother I knew that he was a married man and had a child whom he used to bring along to meet me on the first few weekends when I was in the city and begged him to come over with some home food.

The flat was a modest three-bedroom apartment, which I later went on to share with some of my new friends for a few months, as living alone was getting too boring and monotonous after a while. But for the initial few days, I lived there alone. Jagjeet had arranged a cook and a cleaner for me, who used to frequent the house often, and I ended up befriending them in no time. They were both local boys who told me tales about my new cool city and pointed me in the direction of really cool eating places which served local food. After the initial few days, I decided that I had too much food from outside, because my body started craving for home-cooked north Indian food. Food is the sin that I indulge in more than I should, so I also became best of friends with my cook and made him learn north Indian cooking. He was a quick learner, which was more of a relief for Jagjeet than for me. My cook came in two times a day to prepare food for me. His name was Sanjay, but I preferred to call him 'Chotu', the name he liked to go by.

In the last few days, my life had changed drastically. I had become a student again, which was exciting at first but started to become mundane after a few days as routine sank in. I missed my family and all their love. Long video and audio calls back home became a norm those days. Chotu was my go-to person in Bengaluru as he was always just a call away and knew all about the city, more than all of my friends did put together! His presence in the house made my life in the new city bearable because, to tell the truth, I was really missing Delhi. My parents, however, had moved on quicker than I had anticipated. Last I heard from them, they were to fly to Goa that evening and had already planned three more trips later that year.

My weekends were better spent than the weekdays because during the weekends I was mostly with my friend Bhanu and his partner Pathak at their home nearby. They often had many more people over at their place as well, because they loved hosting parties. Their house was the hub for all their friends. I did make a few new connections in the city, at their home. Back then, I used to drink a little alcohol too. It would be wrong to say that I was not enjoying my free days alone in a new city. Also, a few pegs at parties made me merrier and also a better conversationalist.

I had almost forgotten about Ayra by then; I had nearly forgotten that she even existed. Okay fine! I had not. In fact, after I had sent her the friend request, my mind wandered into the past way too often and managed to recall things and instances which I had completely forgotten about. My brains dug up memories of my friendship with her, some of them hazy, some as fresh as if they had happened just yesterday. Even though she had not accepted my friend request till then, I had rehearsed our first chat, our first phone call, and even our first meeting, not just in my head, but also in front of my bathroom mirror. I can tell you, with a lot of shame of course, that I had rehearsed the much-anticipated meeting in front of the mirror more than a few times and nearly perfected my introduction and a not-so-creepy smile. I was even caught in the act by Chotu twice, who gave me sympathetic looks indicating how worried he was about my mental health.

While she was yet to respond to me on Facebook, I had asked a few old friends from school as well as my college mates back in Delhi to keep an eye out and let me know if anyone gets to know her whereabouts. I was primarily interested in her contact number. But no one had come back with anything.

Studies were as boring as they could be even two weeks later and the only interesting thing that happened in my life was that I had managed to learn how to make tea. I had perfected the art by making cup after cup of the beverage for myself and Chotu, who was not much of a tea lover. That evening, while I was making tea for myself and my overworked and overtired cook, who cooked and cleaned after me and made me feel more like a kid than my mother, I heard a beep on my phone and asked Chotu to fetch the it from wherever it was lying in the house. While taking the sips of the tea, I checked the notification.

It was from her.

She had finally accepted my friend request and I was over the moon because of the virtual connection. I was following her on Instagram, Twitter, and Snapchat within seconds. The messenger on Facebook indicated that she was online and I decided to drop in a non-creepy 'Hi' and wait to see if she went offline to avoid a conversation.

Much to my surprise, she typed 'hello', and that was when I had a brain freeze. All the charming lines I had practised and rehearsed had disappeared from my head, leaving behind a big dark hole. I typed, deleted and retyped a sentence so many times that by the time I finally managed to send her a boring 'how have you been?' she went offline. I never had any trouble talking to any girl in my life, not even to her when we did talk in the past. But since I had last seen her, something had changed. I could not really keep a finger on what exactly it was, but it was definitely something to do with the way she looked now, like a dream to say the least.

With nothing else to do, I invested my precious time searching her account for more information about her life, for hours. Sometime later, I had saved a few of her pictures on my desktop, and was aware that she was at that time working for a bank in Gurgaon as an assistant manager for loans. It appeared that she still lived with her parents and was definitely not married. Her relationship status was hidden and I assumed it to be single, as I was not going to freak her out by asking too many personal questions. There were new stories and posts about her shopping with her sister with hashtags of a wedding. Her sister was soon getting married and Ayra was busy being around her sister, like always, as Somya prepared for her big day.

While waiting for her to come back online again, I decided to not tell her that I had spotted her at the mall the other day and vowed never to mention that I had seen her in the auto in the rain. There was definitely no need to scare her away by telling her that I stalked her online every day since the day she didn't even raise her head to look at me while I gawked at her with my mouth open. After all, there were better things to do in life than scare the poor girl, for example by stalking her online especially now that I had access to all of her accounts and the pictures and tagged places in them. I also did have an assignment to complete for my class the next day but that could wait as she was back online.

Me: You do remember me, right?

Ayra: Of course, I do! Why would I be friends with someone without knowing who they are?

I assumed that she was talking about being friends on Facebook as we were connected there. Though I was friends with people from Czechoslovakia on Facebook just because they had sent a request and we had a few friends in common, I did understand that girls do not just randomly accept a friend or follow request.

Me: Yeah, lol!

That was the best response that I could manage. My brain was stuffed with information about her life and it had a million things running through it, which were more important than thinking of more questions to ask her. It was not really something that my brain cells could work upon at that hour.

Ayra: So, where are you nowadays?

I typed instantly.

Me: Bengaluru, and you?

I knew exactly where she was but then this was a part of the strategy—acting naive and uninformed even though I was by then capable of writing her biography.

Ayra: I am in Bengaluru too!

Bengaluru! Now that was a yorker! I'd never expected her to be in my city; she was supposed to be in Gurgaon with her family. Her sister was getting married soon, so how could she be in Bengaluru? I felt sweat beads appear on my forehead. Why was I freaking out as if she was somewhere nearby?

Is she actually someplace nearby? Does it really matter? She is here; ask her if she wants to meet you. Check where she is. Isn't that the obvious thing to do?

Suddenly my mind was on overdrive.

Me: Really? Where in Bengaluru are you?

I typed as quickly as my head told my fingers to, but then a message appeared on the chat window:

Itsmeayra is offline.

Shit!

I stayed online for hours hoping that she would come back to chat with me but she didn't. I wondered if she was being her old self and it was a prank on me. I didn't want to accept that I had managed to lose a great chance of meeting her while she was in my city. I was sure that she lived in Gurgaon, so there was a possibility of some sort of a joke and I would have liked it to be a joke instead of a missed opportunity, but to my disappointment, it did turn out that she was indeed in Bengaluru that evening. She posted a story on her Instagram tagging a restaurant near my house. I could have sent a response to the story but I didn't want to be so desperate or at least appear to be so desperate. I thought of walking into Orion Mall where the restaurant was but that didn't sound right to my own ears and I decided to wait until she replied to my last message to her. After all, I lived in Rajajinagar and my apartment was hardly a few minutes' drive from where she was having her dinner.

Later that night, as I was beginning to get out of the Romeo mode to start working on my assignment, a ping stopped me from opening my books. She was online again and so was my mother. Mummy was calling on WhatsApp all the way from Goa! I decided to put family over crush and gave all my attention to the conversation with Mummy. The call lasted half an hour and just when I thought that I had missed another opportunity to talk to her I saw that Ayra was still online.

Ayra: I am staying with my sister at Malleshwaram. She works here.

Her response was received sixty-three minutes ago.

That explained it!

Me: Oh, I see. I live in Rajajinagar.

I started hoping that she was still around.

Ayra: I was there a while ago, I guess. I keep getting confused among the names here, lol!

It wasn't funny but I laughed with her. And at my fate!

Soon, she told me all that I knew already about her. She told me where she worked, the college she had completed her studies from, her elder sister Somya's wedding to her American boyfriend, and her living in Gurgaon with her parents. I told her the things that I felt she should know about me now that we were friends. I told her that I was single, living in Bengaluru alone, doing an MBA, and had a secure future planned out. Well, nothing is really planned out in life, I know this now but back then I thought that I had the capability of deciding my own fate. I wish only if I could actually decide my future or even a bit of it, I would definitely place her in my future, as my future!

I do not know whether I was proud of the fact that I was doing an MBA or embarrassed that I was a twenty-six-year-old man who was still studying cluelessly when he should have been helping his ageing father. She was definitely trying to show off her financial independence to me and I found her to be highly motivated in life. She was not like the shy timid Minnie Mouse whom I had met in a school for the first time, even though she looked like one. She was a successful working woman who loved making friends now. She told me how life was too short to be living in the past and I could not have agreed with her more. I loved this new version of her much more than I thought I would. Also, I loved the fact that she didn't care much about me or my family's position in life; she didn't seem to judge me for deciding to study further. She was still the same old Ayra. I felt happy talking to her and grinned the whole time as I typed messages for her to read.

Before it was time for her to sign off again, I took a chance of asking her number.

Me: Do you have WhatsApp?

Ayra: Nope

Me: Okay, I was hoping to ask you for your number on the pretext of communicating through WhatsApp. It is better for chatting than the Facebook messenger.

Ayra: lol

Lol? Why?

Me: Will you still share your number with me? I am so honest after all!

I know I was too cute to say no to, but she did say no to me and gave me a reason which sounded like a lie to me then.

Ayra: I am changing service providers soon. Send me your number and I shall drop in a text when my new number is sorted.

I felt a sharp pang of pain and the bubbles of my feelings seemed to burst. My ego had been hurt and the stupid grin on my face disappeared. Maybe she has a boyfriend who doesn't want her to talk to random boys who try to hit on her, like me. Or maybe her parents still refer to me as the 'brat' who was a bad influence on her, or probably she herself thought of me as a bad influence in her life. The thought train went by making all the noise that it could to stir up some unfamiliar emotions in my heart. But I did send her my number anyway. Sidelining your ego once in a while is okay as long as one is not taken for a ride. After sharing my number with her, we bid each other goodnight. She must have slept while I worked all night on my assignment, which was to be presented the next day.

The next day, I woke up late, just the way I always did. Chotu had the key to the apartment and he had a habit of sneaking into the place like a mouse, every morning. That day, he was almost done preparing my breakfast when I woke up with a jolt. A very loud noise pierced through my ears. It was the fire alarm. I ran out of the bedroom as fast as I could to check what had caught fire in the house. Even though it was a relatively new building with a state-of-the-art infrastructure, there were no working sprinklers or fire extinguishers inside the apartment and one was advised to rely on their own equipment in case of emergencies.

As soon as I stumbled out of the bed and reached the door which opened into the living area, I saw that in the living room, stood a confused Chotu with a long stick in his hand, trying to reach the buttons on the fire alarm. He was only four-feet-six-inches tall! Anyhow, the moment he saw me rush towards him like a maniac, he handed me the stick and said innocently, 'It was the last paratha, bhaiya ji.' He had been making aloo parathas for my breakfast when the alarm went off because like always, he had purposely forgotten to switch on the electric chimeny. This habit of his annoyed me the most and he never learned from his mistakes. A week ago, when the alarm had gone off for the first time because of his cooking, I had learnt how to switch it off with the help of a long stick. I had to press the green button on the alarm for a while before it stopped. Over just a week, I had mastered the art because of five more such instances and Chotu was trying to replicate the same stunt.

I took the stick from his hand grumpily and aimed at the green button on the alarm. I pressed on it for a few seconds for the siren to stop while giving some instructions to my cook. 'Open all the windows and the door and switch the damn exhausts on now!' I told him irritatedly and he did as commanded.

'Sorry bhaiya,' he mumbled in his low voice and I could no longer hold my anger.

'Please switch on the electric chimney as well as the exhaust fans every time you cook, especially when you make parathas.' I was telling him the same thing for the millionth time, fully aware that he was not going to do as told; but just like his *param dharma*—foremost duty—was to ignore my pleas, mine was to plead every time he cooked. After all my words fell on his deaf ears, I gave him a customary smile to say that I was no longer angry and rushed back quickly into the room to take a shower as he had more food to attend to. By the time I took a speedy shower, I was half an hour behind the schedule already!

But I was not late for the first time in my life. I was a veteran at being late every time. Chotu knew that by then. He had already laid out the breakfast table and packed my fruits for the day before I came out to eat. In all the hustle and bustle of the morning, I had no time to look at my phone even once that morning and I asked Chotu to fetch it as I gobbled one paratha. Chotu, my lifeline, used to plug in my phone to charge every morning as soon as he walked into the house as I never did the same. My phone died on me every now and then even in Delhi and was mostly running on low battery.

After wiping away the tones of grease, which had transferred from the paratha onto my hand, I switched on the data on the phone and kept it aside to concentrate again on my fattening and amazingly tasty breakfast. Suddenly, alerts on my phone started making noises and messages and chat heads started pilling one over the other. I moved my eyes towards the screen for a quick second to scan over all that was flashing on my phone's screen.

I smiled and my heart hummed a song. Right there, in front of my eyes on the home screen of my phone was the reason for me bunking classes that day. I was going to call in sick. That was decided before I could even finish relishing the second paratha of the day.

CHAPTER 5

The Much Awaited First Meeting.

Ayra: My sister is out with her friends all day today. Are you free? Wanna catch up?

I re-read the message again after breakfast and contemplated where to take her for our first date. She did not say that it was a date and must have intended it to be a friendly meeting, but in my head, it was a date and I knew I had to make a very good first impression on her. I knew that we were not going to the same mall where she had been to last evening. It would have not only been very boring for her but I did not want her to go to a place she had visited before as I wanted her to see a new place with me. A place that she could associate only with me in Bengaluru; a place that we would later recall as 'our' place.

Also, I could not take her to a place near my college because then the lie of being sick would be busted in no time as most of the professors as well as students loved spending their time outdoors when they were not busy and the mall was not very far away from my college. In my head, I ran over all the other interesting places that I had been to in the city to circle out the one where it was the safest to take her for the first time. It had to be a special place where we could make memories.

Me: Do you like coffee?

I typed hurriedly, and this time, thankfully, I didn't have to wait forever for her response. Unlike me, she did like coffee. So, I decided to take her to a place called 'Matteo Coffea'. It was a coffee house that apparently almost everyone I had met suggested as a 'must-visit' place, but my love for chai always stopped me from going there. I finally had a reason to drop in there and see what exactly the fuss was about.

Me: So, where shall I pick you up from?

Despite all the money that Papa had, he had declined my request to send me my favourite motorbike from Delhi. My love for my 'Dhanno' as I called her, was not hidden from anyone. I loved her more than all the cars my father owned. She was and is number one for me when it comes to vehicles. The 1978 restored Royal Enfield 350cc was the pride of my life. She belonged to my grandfather at one time and was mine since the time I got my license. Papa thought that I should and could manage without Dhanno for the two years that I planned to be in Bengaluru. So there I was in a new city, without any mode of personal transport. Not that I needed one as my college was very close to the place I lived and most days when I had to go somewhere, some or the other acquaintance was there to help. I contemplated if I should ask Jagjeet for his car to pick Ayra up but then realized that he was a working man whom I should not bother over what could have been the only car in his household.

So, after some more careful thinking, I dropped in a text to Pathak, Bhanu's partner, asking him if I could borrow his car instead. Even though I was new to Bengaluru and hardly knew any of the roads, I was fully aware how an auto or Uber was a better idea. But I still didn't want to ruin my first impression. 'It was all about impressions,' I told myself, brushing aside the thoughts around my lack of awareness of the city. A car ride sounded like a safer option as Pathak's new car had an inbuilt GPS to guide me through the roads. While Pathak was cool with me taking his car, Ayra wasn't.

Once Pathak confirmed that I could pick up his car from their home, I texted Ayra to inform her that I would be picking her up in one hour's time and asked her for her hotel's address.

Ayra: Why do you want to pick me up? I shall come on my own. Send me the address of the place you want to meet me at.

When I read her message, my mind read it in her voice from school and somehow, she sounded rude and upset to me. 'Why is she being so rude?' I wondered, 'I was trying to be nice while all she is being is distant.' I did not like her response much and the thought that she was probably not comfortable with me irked me. I was being unreasonable, to say the least. She hardly knew me as an adult and was happy to meet me for coffee and all I could think of was, 'Why so much of mystery? It is not adding any charm, if at all it is doing anything, it is irritating me. She is doing this on purpose.' It was the child in me talking.

Anyhow, no matter how unreasonable and pissed I was, I really did want to meet her so I told her to come over to Matteo Coffea and sent her the address.

Ayra: Okay, see ya in half an hour.

Her reply was to my liking. 'I have cancelled my MBA classes for her so she better be nice to me all day,' I hoped, wished and silently prayed.

Matteo Coffea, Church Street.

I had first heard of the place when I'd gone to Bhanu's house. A few friends of his were discussing how amazing the coffee at this place was. According to them, it was the best place around and a must-visit for all coffee lovers. I am honestly not a very big fan of coffee. I am more of a chai person as I mentioned before, but as soon as I stepped inside the cafe, the place made an impression in my heart. It was indeed very charming and peaceful at that hour. They had plush red sofa seats, which looked very comfortable as well as inviting.

No matter how much I wanted to avoid all the people from my college, I did run into a couple who was cosily chatting at the corner table. They looked as if they were off sick too that day, just like me. I gave them a diffident smile, which they reciprocated. Our eyes met for a fraction of a second and a pact was made—everyone stays mum. No one saw anyone at that place. I occupied the other corner seat and waited for Ayra. A few minutes later, the table next to mine was occupied by some coffee enthusiasts who discussed how an ideal cup of coffee should be handcrafted and how it should be passed through a series of unique and natural processes. With nothing else to do to pass my time, I eavesdropped and tried to memorize all the information that came my way, as I wanted to really impress 'Miss Coffee Lover' who was nowhere to be seen.

One of the coffee lovers summed up his coffee as 'super deliciousness poured into your cup' and I made a note of the phrase on my phone to use it at some point in my conversation with Ayra. For my self-assumed first date, I wore the best casuals I had in my wardrobe—a crisp white shirt with no stains on it and a navy-blue denim. My mother thinks that I look really cute in the combo but then she is my mother and is supposed to think that I am the cutest in the world.

Even though I was already ten minutes late as per the scheduled time when I started off from home and then was even stuck in a tiny little traffic jam as I drove to the coffee house, she was still not there. I hoped that I had not been stood up. When I stepped out of the house late, my strategy was to make her wait, just a little. That is why I had planned to be late by fifteen minutes or so. Much to my disappointment, I was the one who had to wait for her. So, my strategy to make her wait failed to do any good. On the other hand, her strategy, if at all it was strategically planned to make me wait, was working wonders as I was dying to get a glimpse of her.

After the group that was seated right behind me left with their take-away orders, I realized that there were hardly any customers at the place at that hour. I observed a couple of staff members behind the counter and counted the customers in queue waiting for their orders—there were three more people other than me. Rubbing my hands in anticipation of our first date, I looked down at the table. *It was a date!* I just didn't say it out loud to her but it was, at least for me.

I fixed my gaze at the entrance. 'She is not going to come, is she? And you do not even have her contact number,' I thought to myself. My crazy mind can work overtime sometimes.

I started fidgeting with the menu and after a while, I was keenly looking at the beverages they had to offer along with the prices mentioned next to each. This is one middle-class habit that I learned from my parents and wished would never leave me. Everything in the world has a price and one should always be aware of the costs involved, be it money, emotions, time or place in life.

I was looking at the prices attached to the coffee when my concentration broke because of a familiar sound in the background. It was a soft giggle, which I had heard many times in my life. I raised my head to find a customer laughing with the staff behind the counter. It was a girl; her voice was soft and it was definitely not the first time that I was listening to it. I moved my gaze back to the entrance; she was not there yet. So, I moved my eyes back to the menu while my mind and ears drifted in the direction of the giggles.

'Really? You guys make it sound so interesting. Give me a packet of these too. And can I please get a cookie with my coffee? Thanks!' The girl sounded lovely, her voice was like music but I just couldn't turn around and look at her—what if Ayra came in and saw me looking at some other girl? I didn't want to appear to be a loser who was looking out for girls to stare at while waiting for his date. I couldn't just lose my focus like that, could I? Yes, I could, and I did. I turned around to see who was making all that beautiful noise in the coffee shop and there she stood. Ayra had her hands full with packets of what looked like cookies and coffee beans, she also had a cup of coffee and was balancing everything very poorly as she dropped a few packets while looking around to find a comfortable place to sit.

'Hey, hi!' I raised my hand and called out a little too loudly. Immediately, I stood up from my chair and leaped forward to help her with the packets which had fallen on the floor. I was glad that she did not ditch me.

'Hi,' she replied in an audible but soft tone as she looked straight at me. 'I thought you would not come!' She surprised me with her words. 'Me? I wouldn't have come? How was that possible? I had been waiting for days for this to happen,' I wondered.

'Really? Why?' I asked her.

'Yes, I have been at the place for half an hour and when you didn't turn up I thought of leaving with my take-away order,' she told me looking at all the stuff which she and I had placed on the table by then. 'If you wouldn't have seen me and called out to me, I would have walked out of the door,' she told me. I wondered how I had missed spotting her when I had in fact scanned the place as soon as I walked in and I could swear that she was not there then. 'I have been here for a while and I did check the place entirely when I came in. I swear I didn't see you or else I would have walked up to you,' I told her truthfully.

She raised both her shoulders and cocked her head, 'Maybe you walked in when I was in the washroom. That explains it, in fact,' she told me and took the first sip of her coffee. 'Hmmm . . . sorry!' she exclaimed almost instantly and then added, 'What would you like to have? I am sorry I brought only one coffee.' She was apologizing for nothing and that was the moment when I realized that she had, on her own brought her coffee when it was supposed to be a date and like a gentleman, I intended to get her anything that she needed. Well, that train had passed and I had nothing else to do than to excuse myself and get something to eat.

'What would you like to have?' she asked me again. 'Let me have a look at what all they have to offer,' I lied to her. I had seen the menu already and I knew exactly what I wanted to have. I ordered their signature drink, the Shekaratos. Once we sat down, I saw her as I had never seen her before. The image of her sitting at the table with her hair tied back in a ponytail and several loose strands of soft hair brushing her cheeks is still fresh in my memories. Even today, when I close my eyes and think of our first coffee date, I see her sitting by the same wall, dressed in a peach top that had shiny details on it. With every movement of hers, they reflected light on her face and made her sparkle too. She didn't seem to be bothered by the countless reflections on her. Her nerdy glasses were missing that day. She appeared to have been wearing contact lenses as she was not adjusting her vision every now and then; she did that when she was neither wearing glasses nor contacts.

Her face shone and her porcelain fair skin looked smooth like nothing had ever touched it. She smiled nervously at me while I adjusted myself in the seat opposite her. Even though we were seated right under an AC vent, her smile made me warm. The way she looked at me as she spoke, I felt a calmness sweep over me. The image of her beautiful face was imprinted somewhere deep in my heart.

I felt her making a place inside my heart for herself where she would live forever.

I felt her become a part of who I was to become with her.

In less than a few minutes, the girl who was looking down at her hands in her lap again and again changed into a chatter-box. A different version of her leaped out of her and she spoke for endless hours about her discussion with the barista. As much as I was keen to know more about her, I was also keen at staring at her. While she spoke, I just smiled at her and made mental notes on small details about her, '. . . You know, some of their coffee is grown in the spice, citrus and vanilla plantations, so this coffee house does take its coffee seriously. There is a plethora of coffee varieties on the menu, with flavour profiles, as well . . . ' She had very little makeup on, just something in her eyes and a lip gloss, which was so inviting. But it was our first meeting and so I had to behave; I had to let her know me. I had to know more about her too and we had to fall in love. 'But I am in love already! She isn't, most likely. It can be a long time before she falls in love with me. I cannot scare her.' I told myself.

So, curbing all the attraction that was pulling me towards her and pouring ice cold water on the sparks that

I felt flying between us, I concentrated on her chatter. She was talking about some of the most amazing coffee houses in the world. One of them was in Sydney and she told me that she was hoping to visit it soon.

'Are you even listening?' she snapped her fingers in front of my face—maybe I was gawking at her; most likely I was.

'Yes, yes I was listening to you, but honestly, I do not really enjoy coffee or coffee talk for that matter.' If we had to know each other better, we had to be honest. That was not the best time to be honest but I couldn't help it. She was just too passionate about coffee. That was the moment I decided to be honest with her forever as lies and deceit has no place in love. This was a promise I made to myself and have never broken.

'I am sorry,' she told me looking as if I had just asked her to kill her pet rabbit.

'Don't be sorry.' I stretched out my hand to comfort her and realized that I shouldn't have done it because as soon as I put my hand on hers she slid her hand away from mine. 'Now I am sorry,' I said awkwardly and she laughed a funny laugh. I had to join in. My Shekaratos had arrived and I felt the need to get something to eat with it.

'I shall go and order something to eat as well. Do you need anything else?' I was hoping she would say yes but she didn't. It was our first date and she had paid for all her food. I had made her feel awkward by trying to hold her hand and I was once again going to leave her alone at the table with tons of food in front of her. I was not very happy with the way things were going.

'No, I have all that I need right here,' she giggled again and I couldn't contain mine either.

I came back to the table with a plain croissant and a cinnamon roll. She was almost done with her coffee by then.

While talking to her, with mostly her doing the talking and me being the great listener that I always was with her, I noticed that she was not carrying a phone, which was a relief as it meant that she was not lying. We spoke a little about our school days. She remembered fewer things than me and was keener to talk about the present than the past. The trouble was, I had nothing interesting happening in my present and my past was way better than my life at that moment. In fact, meeting her was the most 'happening' thing to have happened to me recently. I asked her about her sister's wedding plans—a relatively safer topic to touch, and this allowed her to talk a lot again. I listened and froze the moment in my memories.

We sat there for more than a couple of hours, and at one o' clock, when I proposed lunch, she disappointed me by telling me that she already had plans to meet her sister and a friend for lunch. After knowing the adult version of her only for a few hours, I knew that she was not lying to me. She was a busy girl who had too much on her plate then. I respected her honesty and was happy that she took time out to meet me.

'It was lovely catching up with you!' she told me, extending her hand for a handshake. I was hoping for a hug but then a handshake was not a bad start either.

'I can drop you wherever you are headed,' I offered in an attempt to prolong our time together.

'I will manage.' Another one of my requests was declined. I took her outstretched hand in mine and that was the first time we touched each other, in a friendly way of course, but it was enough to send shivers down my spine. Surprisingly, for her petite frame she had a very firm handshake and her palms were not overtly soft like most girls that I have shaken hands with. She looked straight into my eyes as if trying to look through them and reach out to my soul. I held her gaze to find what I had been missing for years, I wanted to see what she felt for me. I could not find love in her eyes; they had something deeper in them, they looked lovely and yet one could tell that underneath all the beauty was something that she was trying hard to hide. But I did realize that it was not love that she was trying to hide, she had deeper secrets.

Even though she had no love in her eyes for me then, I did—I had lots and lots of love already oozing out of me, and my face reflected that in crimson. I was blushing like crazy and the girl in front of me was looking at me like I was a monkey in observation.

Even though everything about her oozed confidence, I did notice that she had sweaty palms. 'Maybe she is nervous too but does a great job at hiding it,' I wished.

'Till when are you in Bengaluru?' I asked her, not leaving her hand, which I shook lightly as we talked.

'I leave tonight,' she told me, abruptly looking down at our intertwined hands and I let go of her.

'Here, I forgot to give you these,' she was about to embarrass me further. She dipped her hand into her large white tote and pulled out a big box of assorted Ferrero

Rocher. 'I remembered they were your favourite,' she added. *They are my favourite, have always been my favourite.* Papa used to get boxes of Ferrero Rocher whenever he visited Europe and I used to carry them to school to share them with Ayra. She remembered, which was awesome, but I had got nothing for her. I couldn't say 'no' to her gift as at some point there was a chance to hear a 'no' for mine if I declined the present then. So, I turned scarlet at the visible lack of manners from my end.

'I am sorry, I didn't get you anything . . .' I had to say shamelessly as I accepted her gift.

'No worries, brat! It's all good,' she said to me patting my shoulder with a wink. She was a buddy and I felt at ease.

We accompanied each other till the parking lot, where I walked towards the loaned car while she stood at a place to hail an auto. I wanted to turn around and wave goodbye and see her smile one last time but that would have gone against the strategy, so I didn't. I wanted her to feel what I had begun feeling before I made my feelings obvious to her. And that required patience. Till then, we were 'just friends'!

She had to take a flight which took her back to Delhi in the evening and then at night after she reached home we resumed our chatting on Instagram and Facebook messenger. In the initial few days, I itched to ask her if she was single but soon I realized that I didn't want to know her relationship status anymore. It was probably because I was scared that she was not. A girl who was pretty, confident, funny and caring had to be with someone—someone who was better than me; someone who knew exactly what he wanted in his life.

But my feelings for her had escalated really quickly from attraction to infatuation to level one of love. At that stage, to know that she had a boyfriend was going to hurt my heart badly. In fact, the thought of being with her forever had started making space in my idle mind by the end of the first month while she had not even hinted at any interest in me.

Our chats lasted hours and I realized that even though I had moved on to make more than a few friends after she disappeared from my life suddenly, no one matched up to her. I realized how we were each other's first friends, and first friendships are deeper than most bonds in the world. She cracked jokes as no one else did and I wondered what her laughter sounded like in the silence of the night when she and I would be together under the stars. Her smile was infectious and yet a strange feeling kicked me in the gut every time I recalled her smiling—her smile was perfect but her eyes remained sad even when she smiled.

While I suffered a little because I was getting to know her better too slowly for my liking, my studies suffered because she took her time to reply to most of my messages, and I, like a fool, stared at my phone screen while she typed and retyped, all the while completely ignoring my studies.

To no one's surprise, I struggled really hard to keep up with my studies at college but I didn't want to choose between being with her, and my studies. I wanted to do both, and when you really want to do something, a force helps you cope up with all the adversities. The force that came to inspire me was my lecturer who threatened to call my family. So, I managed both with less sleep but complete concentration.

Everything was smooth but small blunders kept happening again and again shaking my confidence. Like one Sunday, while chatting with her on Facebook, I accidentally hit the video call button and to my surprise, she picked up. At that moment, it was as if my brain had accidentally taken a vacation. I tried to say something but nothing came out of my mouth except air. I saw her face light up my laptop's screen as she tilted her head and looked puzzled. It appeared as if she too had accidentally answered the call. She parted her lips and chewed on the lower lip. This was the moment my screen froze and the connection was lost.

'Phew!' a small sigh escaped my lips.

Ayra: Did you just call?

I saw her message blink on my phone after a while and the screen on my laptop was still frozen with her picture on it.

Me: I don't know what happened. I must have pressed the call button mistakenly. I am sorry.

I was clumsy and now my secret was out in the open.

I again moved my focus towards the frozen screen. She looked cute, to say the least, in her nerdy glasses and Disney printed tee. After getting to know her all over again, I found her many times more beautiful than I did when I saw her at the mall.

Ayra: Why sorry? It is all right. You apologize too much!

This was the last message from her for the night and I wondered if she was angry with me. I didn't have a lot of time to ponder over it as it was almost midnight and I had not yet begun studying for my tests the next day.

CHAPTER 6

September 2017

After that video call blunder, nothing much happened between Ayra and me for a while. I was occupied with my studies a bit and she was busy with her sister's wedding. Also, I was too cautious while chatting with her via the laptop. A few 'Good morning' and 'How are you?' messages on Facebook are all that I can trace on my chat history from those days. I remember the period as a sad and melancholic phase in my life in general because my mother had fallen ill and I was very worried about her health for many days. I was spending my weekends in Delhi at home with my parents and all the travelling took a toll on my general well-being. My studies now seemed to be a burden on my family and I felt this the most.

I was actually zoned out until she fully recovered. But the twenty-fifth day of September 2017 brought with it some really good news for me. Mummy was finally fully recovered from the mysterious flu which had caused her to lose seven kilos and had resulted in many visits to the hospital. Also, I received an 'Independence Day' text message from an unknown number. I have a habit of saving all unknown numbers as 'Who' on my phone and then changing the name of the contact once their identity has been established. This unknown number or 'Who' was Ayra's. She sent me another message moments after I had saved the contact as 'Who' to tell me it was her and I quickly renamed the contact as 'Ayra S'. I do not remember exactly what the intent was—probably to signify that the number belonged to Ayra Sharma or a way to attach my initials to her name and refer to her as Ayra Sahil. But as I said, I do not remember the exact reason why I had suffixed the S. That mobile number is still saved as Ayra S on my phone.

So, it was finally settled in my head that she had not been lying about her phone number situation. Initially, when she had told me about changing her mobile number, I wondered if we were ever going to be on calls with each other, like typical lovers all over the world who cling to their phones at every given opportunity. There I had it—I had my opportunity. Now all I had to do was ensure that we did become lovers in our real lives and not just in the wonderland of my head.

That day she reappeared on social media too and one after the other she posted snaps and videos of her sister's wedding. I congratulated her for Somya's wedding and spent the rest of the day liking her pictures and saving them on my phone. In the evening when she called me for the first time, she told me that her sister was finally off to America to live with her new family and then asked me how my life had been. I did not want to bother her with my mother's health or my troubles at college but I was emotionally weak and broke down as soon as she asked me how things were at college. Ayra was a compassionate listener—a quality of hers that I admire the most. We chatted at length about my family and I might have spoken more than she did to be honest, but she didn't appear to mind it and I could tell that because of the way she sounded. She sounded 'genuinely interested' in everything that I told her. Right from the fact that I had been bunking lectures and indulging in more alcohol than I had ever had, to the scare that I got when I saw my mother on the hospital bed. She made me promise that when Mummy is healthy and back home, I would quit alcohol for good.

'I will, I promise,' I told her instantly even when I knew that it was going to be really tough.

But that was the first thing ever she had asked me to do and I could not have let her down. Let me also add that not a single drop of alcohol went down my throat after our call that evening. I am not even a social drinker anymore—I quit for her.

Her parents were away that evening and she was all alone at home. This was the reason we could talk over the phone. 'This will not be possible on other days as my parents really do not like me talking to boys as such,' she told me and I wondered why.

'Sure, we can talk when you are at work,' I suggested, fully aware that at the time of the day when she was at work I was supposed to be at college.

'I can take only a few calls at work,' she explained to me and it was agreed upon that we should talk when she travelled to and from work.

'Once back home, I am supposed to be off the phone,' she spoke like a school teacher and I told her that I shall call her only when she would be available to take the call. I also made a mental note that my texts will not be answered immediately after five and I should not let my mind overthink when this happens. After about a couple of hours, her phone's battery died. So, after plugging in her phone to charge, we started texting each other instead. There was so much to talk about and we had such a small window to talk to each other. It was all thrilling and kind of cute. While chatting with her over texts, I picked up a topic which I otherwise would not have spoken about. It was the difficult topic of 'I liked you more than a friend.'

Me: So, do you remember the time in school when Smriti told you that I liked you? Like 'liked you' liked you. Are you still upset over that?

I was not really looking forward to my stay in Bengaluru anymore, especially after my mother's health had deteriorated. I had Pathak and Bhanu's company in the city and I also had Chotu, but then these people had their own lives to be busy with and I was not the centre of anyone's universe. Coming to the city was my decision and so was taking up the MBA course, but who says one has to stand by all the decisions one takes.

Sometimes, you make mistakes in judging what you actually want and once you figure out what exactly you want from life, no matter what decisions you have made in the past, you should not stop yourself from altering your life's course. I had figured that I wanted to live with my family, get married, grow old with a woman like Ayra, have kids, become a successful entrepreneur like my father, take my father's business to new heights, and work on my book, but the MBA did not fit the new life plan anymore. Now that her elder sister was married, I knew that her parents would soon start looking for a match for her too. So, I had to act fast. Honestly, I have a very orthodox mental set-up. By then I knew that I was in love with her and that to start living with her was the next obvious step. And to be able to spend my life with her, I had to marry her.

Ayra: Nope, why would I be upset about it?

She responded to my liking.

Me: Good! So, you are okay with the fact that I like you more than a friend, right?

I drew a deep breath and clicked the send button.

Ayra: I am sorry. I overreacted; I shouldn't have called you a brat. I knew how much you hated that word then.

She completely ignored my question but I was happy and felt light to have conveyed my feelings to her. It was much needed at that point. 'Baby steps, one step at a time,' I told my racing heart.

Me: I still do. But I forgive you, for I am too cute. And you called me a 'stupid brat' by the way.

I could not help type the last bit. Later that evening, I asked her what exactly her work was like and how far she was in terms of her book, and she happily narrated some really awesome tales from her work. Every time we connected, I realized that her life was so eventful, while I was basically a potato compared to her.

Then one evening, at around seven in the evening, I got a call from my mother's number. She called me to let me know that a friend of mine had come over to visit her. I wondered who it was as I had hardly spoken about her health with any of my friends in Delhi. Being a pro at using all WhatsApp features, she quickly changed the call type from audio to video and I saw the pretty girl sitting beside Papa and chatting with him at a distance. Mummy was in the lobby while the duo sat in the living room.

It was Ayra.

To my surprise, Ayra had decided to spend her free evening with my mother and father as I was away, and honestly, nothing in the world could have been more perfect than this girl. My mother winked at me as she moved the camera back towards herself and thus my love life was the talk of my household now. Without any questions from my mother, I confessed that I loved this girl and wanted to marry her, but Mummy could not tell her—not yet.

Some days later . . .

My parents sleep exactly at eleven every night and Ayra, too, never stayed up late after bidding me goodnight around twelve. For any late-night emergencies, I had requested all my friends and family members to call me on my landline only, as I liked to switch off the internet on my mobile phone every night and put it on silent mode before I go to bed. This is my way of detoxifying my life from the cellular clutter every day. I must also add that this wasn't my idea. There is a 'no cell phone in the bedroom' policy at my parent's house and I have just taken it a step further by putting the mute button on my phone to minimize distraction. It has worked wonders for me since I started the practice and I recommend it to everyone who is kind of addicted to scrolling unnecessarily all night, every night. Nothing is more precious than a well-rested and rejuvenated mind, and a good night's sleep gives you exactly that.

That morning as soon as I connected my mobile phone to the internet, like every other morning, my cell phone went crazy as it beeped with numerous alerts. The world of social media never sleeps—someone checks in somewhere in the world and Facebook thinks that it is very important that I am always informed as soon as it happens. Ignoring the tons of beeps and tings on my phone, I headed to the bathroom. It was a Sunday, which meant it was laundry day for me. I had taken up the task of doing my own laundry twice a week, once on Wednesday and once on Saturday. It was my attempt at trying to see how well I would fair in a domesticated life; not that I would have to wash my clothes, but this gave me a sneak peek into the responsibilities I was dying to take up. And to be honest, I was killing it. I loved doing the chores, and while at work, I used to be relaxed and somehow more focused.

It was eight-thirty when I walked back into my bedroom. Chotu was making some delicious breakfast in the kitchen, thankfully with the exhausts switched on. My phone was finally not beeping any more, though I could see an occasional green light on the top of the screen flashing up indicating that a lot had been downloaded on it. I do not really detest social media; after all, it did help me track down Ayra. But I am definitely not one of its biggest admirers either. It is a lot of unnecessary information, which occupies space in our heads when there is no need for it. We are becoming an overtly informed generation that doesn't know what to do with all the information being thrown our way, which not everyone requires.

Yet, I do have accounts on all major social media platforms. 'Why do you have accounts on Instagram, Facebook, Snapchat etc.?' you would ask. The answer is simple—peer pressure. The feeling of being left out, of missing out if we are not doing exactly what others are doing and this is the worst feeling of all. Most importantly, I have these accounts because all my friends from school and college have moved to different cities, some even to different countries and this is the easiest way to be in touch with everyone, now that calling and texting are so passé.

While my phone readily presents me with all the information from across the world, I follow what my Dadu, my paternal grandfather, had once told me: 'Be like a gannet.' It is an Australian diving bird that dives into the ocean, picks up the fish it wants to pick and dashes out of the water, all in ten seconds flat.

So, I picked my phone and started scanning the updates, categorizing the important ones and the I-do-not-care ones. Though I can never really dive into the world of my phone and come out with what I need in ten seconds, I do manage to scroll through a lot, very fast. My fingers stopped scrolling at a not-very-useful update which had to be responded to. A friend's friend had moved to America. 'Congratulations!' I typed hastily and moved on.

In approximately fifteen minutes, I was done with WhatsApp, Instagram, Facebook, and my emails. 'Done for the day!' I told myself. Since Ayra was going to be busy with her own household chores for the first part of the weekend, there was nothing else to do. This was the norm for her and she followed it religiously every weekend. Suddenly, her name appeared on top of my screen. It was a birthday reminder from Facebook: 'Ayra Sharma has her birthday on Wednesday. Help her make her day special.' Hell yes!

I smiled thinking of our birthdays when we were kids. She hardly ever celebrated her birthday while I always did. On her birthdays, I gave her small presents even when she insisted that her mother would not like it. I generally enjoy gifting even though I must confess that I am not very good at planning surprises. In school, Ayra's presents used to be small things—pens, pencil cases, greeting cards, etc. Life was so simple back then. Thinking of the innocent days, I felt my face warm up. I started typing a thoughtful 'happy birthday' message on her wall when it struck me—it was her twenty-fifth birthday. I gave out a squeal of delight.

I typed a neat message to her: 'Wishing you a very happy twenty-fifth birthday! So, tell me, where and when?'—and saved it to my drafts.

CHAPTER 7

Wednesday
27 September 2017

I hit the send button on the message in my drafts folder. It was her twenty-fifth birthday and I expected her to be with her family, as it was an occasion when your family gets to pamper you and treat you like a star just for being born on that particular day. It is funny because we make absolutely no contribution to our birth. It is to do with our parents initially and then all the labour is done by our mums, who are not celebrated enough. Anyhow, with her sister moving overseas after her wedding, I was not really hoping to get a quick reply from the birthday girl, as I expected her to be pampered doubly by her parents that year to fill the void. I did hope to be able to talk to her at least once that day but I knew that she never called when her 'mummy and daddy', as she referred to her parents, were around.

Taking me by surprise the usual Ayra way, she responded almost immediately, 'I thought you would have forgotten. Thanks! What is this where and when?'

As I read her reply, my idiot grin came instantly back on my face. 'Can I call?' I asked her.

'Yes, after an hour? Sorry, can't take a call right now,' she proposed.

'Yeah, sure,' I said happily. I hummed and sang and resumed my daily chores. Chotu stared at me funnily as I wriggled my hips and danced to my own off-tune tracks with missing lyrics. Then as soon as one hour was over, I messaged her again to check if we could talk.

'Yep,' she replied.

I immediately pressed the green call button as I walked over to the balcony. I expected her to be talking in whispers so that she was not heard by her parents. I wondered why she was so scared of them, mostly because I adored my parents and they were more like friends to me. I could not imagine that any other sort of parent-child relation could exist. I was so wrong! I know that now—there are more than many types of relationships in this world; in fact, every relationship is unique.

As soon as she picked up the call I heard an announcement in the background. I could tell that she was in the metro. 'Are you going somewhere with your family?' I asked her after wishing her once again.

'I am going to the office, Mister. Some people have to work for a living!' she taunted.

I let it pass. It was her birthday after all. 'Why? It is your birthday!' I reminded her, just in case she had forgotten that one is not supposed to work on their birthdays. 'Who works on their birthday?' I asked her again when she didn't respond to my last question.

'I do,' was her dry response, and she went quiet again. I was at a loss of words myself and there was an awkward pause as I waited for her to tell me why. There had to be more to it.

'My parents went to attend a family function in Meerut last night. They will be back tomorrow. What can a person do sitting alone at home, so I decided to go to work instead? I anyhow have worked during all three of my birthdays since I joined this office,' she told me as if stating a fact, but I could sense the sadness in her voice. I had planned to pull her leg about this as it was her twenty-fifth birthday and also remind her of our pact to get married if we didn't meet anyone else. But her situation demanded a different conversation. I could not help but feel funny in my stomach.

This was not right. She should not be working on her birthday. We had never really spoken about our relationship status till that moment, and I did not want to invade her privacy by trying to ask her if she was single or not and she had never really shown any interest in my love life either. This was the first time she had mentioned that she was single, and with no boyfriend in the picture, my mind started painting me as her knight with a shining armour, but whether or not she needed one was another question. I wanted to be there for her birthday. I wanted her to be happy on the day when she was supposed to be the happiest ever. She, like everyone else, had to pretend to be cheerful about growing old and inching towards the end. I knew how my family and friends made such a big deal about each and every birthday to make the person feel special and I wanted her to feel the same way. This was the Malhotra way!

'Are you crazy? Twenty-five is a milestone!' I told her.

'Ha ha ha . . . ' she faked a laugh that made her sound sadder.

That is it. I am going to be with her. After all, even my Papa and Mummy were off to Dehradun for a break to help Mummy recover. Going to Delhi in their absence was safe. There was no way anyone could catch me sneaking in without informing the family as long as I stayed away from south Delhi, Noida and Gurgaon.

That didn't leave much of Delhi for me to roam around in, but that was the way it was and I made peace with it. Before my mind burst in anticipation, I popped the question to her, 'Do you want to meet me today?' I asked her this mustering all the courage that was hiding in the corners of my heart. She usually didn't want me to come over at very short notices. She wanted to be no trouble at all in anyone's life.

'I cannot come to Bengaluru,' she stated the obvious like a child.

'I know. I was planning to come over and meet you.' Just last night I had been telling her so much about my studies making her believe that I was doing something amazing and couldn't even spare a minute for anything else. I was lying, of course—studies were the last thing on my mind and by then, my parents had got a hint of it too. They liked Ayra and had met her two more times since she visited

Mummy at my home. Papa had been hinting at my return to Delhi and getting settled as well.

'No, don't do that. I am used to being alone on my birthdays. I am not a big fan of all the unnecessary drama around celebrating birthdays. I hope you understand.' No, I did not understand. I did not want to understand either. No matter what she had been saying, I started doing my calculations. With so many flights that I took in the last month, I knew at the top of my head that if I took the 11 a.m. flight, I would be in Delhi by lunchtime.

I didn't try to make her believe that I was serious about being with her that day. My actions were to speak louder than any of my words. She reached her office and the call ended. I got dressed, called a cab and dashed towards the airport in no time. Despite keeping Ayra in a loop about each and every move of mine—right from hailing a cab to the airport to alighting the flight—she didn't believe me, until I was standing outside her office building, with a bouquet. I liked roses the most and assumed that she liked them the most too. After all, who doesn't like roses—they are the best and there are so many colours to choose from! I chose a bouquet with roses of three colours in it—yellow, pink and red. It was the most beautiful bouquet in the flower shop at the airport. It turned out that Ayra was allergic to roses and her favourite flowers were sunflowers, which was the most uncommon choice to be the winner of 'favourite flowers'.

'Why do you like sunflowers?' I was actually amazed at her choice and asked her after we had dropped the flowers which I had brought for her, at her office's reception desk because Ayra couldn't stay anywhere near them.

'I do not know,' she shrugged her shoulders but I insisted that she give me a reason as we headed out of the building. 'Maybe because they always look towards the brighter side of the world?'

'Hmmm . . . ' I scratched my chin absorbing what she said. She had a way with words. Later in my life, I got to know why looking at the brighter side of the world was so important to her and these words made more sense to me.

I was so engrossed with looking at the birthday girl that I did not remember much about her office. One thing that I did notice about her office was that even though the board on top of the high-rise corporate building at InfoCity read the name of a multinational bank, there were no customers allowed in it. I was stopped by the guards at the big reception and was asked to wait there. I had to ask her why the bank where she worked was so much different from a traditional bank. Her office was on the fifth floor and I knew that she preferred taking the stairs to the elevators. That gave us a lot of time to chit-chat.

'Your office doesn't look like a traditional bank,' I commented, as I knew that she was very passionate about her work and would be happy to elaborate.

'Because it is not. I work for the backend team. It is like when you apply for a loan at a branch and they say, "We have sent the application and now we shall get in touch with you if we need something else upon verification." We are the team that does the verification for our bank's customers and we are the ones who decide whether or not a loan should be sanctioned,' she explained moving her hands animatedly.

I did not completely understand all that she told me, but I did get the gist of it and that was enough. I noticed that she slid her hand down the railing as we walked down the stairs and was wearing a thin anklet in her left leg. Some tiny beads in it made a lovely sound, and as we were the only ones there, I could hear them clearly. Anklets did suit her and I made a mental note of it. I was going to gift her a pair one day soon, but on that particular day, I had another gift to worry about.

In a hurry to catch the first available flight, I had skipped buying a present for her since Delhi had 'better' and 'known' options as per me. But I had to tread carefully as I didn't want to be caught by my friends or any of my relatives while I was in Delhi. I proactively called as many people as I could to learn about their whereabouts and plans for the day. I was travelling incognito and went to the extent of making notes to avoid all those places where my people could be found. In my head, I was a spy.

'Where do you want to go for lunch?' I asked her, while I was booking an Uber for us. Ayra had taken the rest of the day off from work.

'I don't know,' was her boring response. I could tell that she wasn't enjoying all the attention from me on her birthday. 'She better get used to this,' I thought.

'I hope you haven't had lunch,' I said, looking at her with a broad smile and she signalled 'no'. 'Let me take you to a very special place then,' I said, and typed the drop location as Khan Market. Things would now have to move as per my plan!

Our ride arrived in less than a minute and our driver Ramesh greeted us with a Mentos and a toothy smile. I let her sit first and then sat next to her and closed the door. The cab had a funny smell but the driver's smile made me not complain about it. The decision to hire a cab instead of picking up one of my friend's car or bike was made by me so that we could travel with no stress of being seen by anyone and also because evenings were now getting colder in Delhi and I had no intentions of dropping her back home before her office hours ended just because it was too chilly outside. After all her parents were not home and what would she have done alone at home apart from wasting the rest of her evening? I checked if my plan worked for her and she told me that she was in no rush to head back home.

'I will just end up sitting alone and wasting my time scrolling through my phone.' she added, almost reading my mind.

Just fifteen minutes after feeling proud of my planning, I realized that the cab had turned into more of a liability than an asset. We had hit the main road some time ago and yet not moved more than a few metres in the heavy traffic. My understanding was that usually, office hours were peak hours in Gurgaon, but I was so wrong.

'You know what, I would have preferred to go on a bike,' she told me, looking out at the endless queue of cars ahead of us. I kind of agreed as I would have preferred a bike ride as well. Part One of my plans for her birthday was officially a failure!

Ayra had eaten her breakfast quite early in the morning and had forgotten to pick up her box of nuts which she carried everywhere with her, at her desk. Her stomach started growling soon and I figured that we would have to eat somewhere nearby instead of going all the way to Khan Market. The cab moved at a snail's pace and I located a McDonald's on our way. It was nearly impossible to do a drive-through at that time, so we bid Ramesh goodbye and got off our ride.

The second part of my plan was to treat her at one of my favourite restaurants in Delhi. I had called a friend and booked a section for her at the restaurant so that we could talk in peace. I wanted to hear her talk as her voice sounded like a melody to my ears. But with us walking into that McDonald's, the second part of the plan came down crashing as well.

Never mind, there is still that gift,' I told myself, just before she said, 'Let's go to Dilli Haat.'

What? Who goes to Dilli Haat on their birthday? Apparently, she wanted to, and her impulsive desire was not to be ignored that day—it was her day and all her wishes were my command. Also, by then I felt that I had somehow managed to make her birthday much worse than she had anticipated by being at work. She had to endure an endless Uber ride, and food from a fast food restaurant where kids screamed and shouted so much that I could hardly understand what she said. The least I could do now was to agree with her.

'Okay,' I said and just like that, the third surprise went down the drain, as her birthday gift was with my friend who was waiting for us at Khan Market. I could have called him over; in fact, I would have to. But the processor in my head begins to slow down when situations run out of control. I told my friend to abort the mission as the Beauty and her Beast were headed somewhere else.

I dropped in a quick message of cancellation to him, apologizing as much as I could. 'Let us take an auto from here,' Ayra suggested and stretched out her right hand to signal an auto. I had indeed seen more than a few auto rickshaws overtake us when we were in the car and gave in to the idea. Honestly, I had no other choice but to agree with her as autos were a better mode of travelling than a car in the standstill traffic which we had to cross to get to Delhi. An auto stopped at the other side of the road. She held the right sleeve of my shirt—not my arm, just the sleeve—and we crossed the road together to secure our space in the auto. It was four in the late afternoon by then and nothing romantic had happened because all my plans were coming down, crashing one after the other.

Once in the auto, it took me only a few minutes to realize the beauty of it all. I was with the girl I liked, and she and I were headed to this place where I had never been to. It was her birthday and she sat so close to me that I could smell her hair. She smelled like cherries with a hint of mint. Her long loose hair that she kept brushing off her face touched my palms often. They were soft like a rabbit's fur! I can vouch for that as I did have a rabbit when I was growing up and it was the softest thing ever.

She and I were coincidentally wearing clothes of the same colour. I was wearing a yellow t-shirt and she, a yellow top and a long white skirt. As she spoke to me about how happy she was to see me and that what I did was the most beautiful thing anyone had ever done on her birthday, I could see her happiness through her eyes and I grinned from ear to ear like a monkey on drugs.

In an auto that zoomed in and out of traffic, we managed to reach our destination sooner than expected. 'This is my favourite place!' she spread her arms wide open as if claiming ownership of the place as soon as we got down outside the main gate. I wanted to look past her to understand what was so magical about the place but I couldn't take my eyes off her. She looked like a sculpture, a piece of art—magnificent, undefinable, surreal and mysterious. Her hair as it bathed in the light of the setting sun shone like a glossy layer of brown silk; her skin was smooth and unblemished and her body reflected joy like it meant to dance. She beamed happily and looked at me, and as I was captivated by her infectious smile. I was a slave of her happiness forever and after.

People tell you that love happens in one moment, at 'one sight', and the truth is that it actually does! Whether that moment is going to be the first moment when you see her or the hundredth, it cannot be predicted by anyone, but it will happen in one single moment. That much I know from experience. And that was the moment when I felt her charm completely bewitch me. She was probably just an ordinary girl who was going gaga over an ordinary place; she was probably just a small girl in a big city, but to me, she was as bright as the sun and she was all that I wanted to be around. Her happiness and enthusiasm made me question things in me, and I liked that. She was the example of people who find happiness in small things—she did that all the time. Dressed in those plain clothes, standing with her head tilted on the left and her arms on her hips as if she owned the place,

Ayra was a picture straight out of my dreams. That was the moment when I truly and madly, fell in love with her. That was the moment I realized what exactly falling in love was!

Mimicking her head tilt, I followed her inside where we were both got frisked by security personals, and then were let in. 'I have never been here before,' I told her honestly, marvelling at the things around me.

'I will show you around then!' she said, holding my hand and pulling me towards her. Then, she snuck her arm under mine, taking me by surprise with that show of intimacy. With that we began our journey. There was way too much to look at and absorb with all the kiosks and stalls of handicrafts strewn all around in a circle. I saw baskets, durries, clothes, small handicraft items . . . the place was a riot of colours and a variety of things. Ayra kept talking non-stop about how pretty this or that was and how she found the place very relaxed, unlike a shopping centre or a movie theatre. 'Relaxed places,' I noted, as this was what I had to keep in mind when I planned something again for her. And also, I vowed to go to a temple before the date so that no more bloopers happen. Only God could save my dates. We moved along several lanes that had handicraft stores on both sides. There were handicrafts from all over the country and the view was indeed fascinating. It was her birthday and I was yet to give her a present, I could not let her go back without something. She went away to look for a washroom and this was when I found something that I thought was made just for her.

Swiftly, I paid for the gift and placed the packet in my backpack. As I was taking back the leftover change for the shopkeeper, I felt her tap on my shoulder. 'Are you buying something from here?' she asked, looking around the shop full of silk clothing.

'No, I just needed some change,' I lied smoothly and we stepped out looking for a place to sit and talk.

Her being a vegetarian, we were forced to sit at a restaurant which served south Indian food. Why 'forced'? Well, because I wanted to have 'Lucknow ke kebab'. Honestly, her being a vegetarian was not a deal-breaker for me as long as she was okay with my not being a vegetarian, which I later got to know that she was okay with. That evening sitting in the small open restaurant, with two cups of filter coffee and two plates of 'medhu vada' in front of us, we talked about a lot of things. I mentioned to her a few times how much we had in common apart from our food preferences and she agreed with me. I felt that we were very compatible. I did thank her for her visits to my house to keep my mother company when she was unwell.

'You do not have to say thank you for this. You know how much I adore your mother, and she likes me as well,' she said with a smile on her face and I couldn't agree more—Mummy did like her a lot and I was glad to know that Ayra 'adored' my mother.

'We are alike in many ways, so maybe you could adore me as well,' I said cheekily.

'How so?' she asked, placing her palm under her chin and resting her elbow on the table, waiting for me to elaborate.

'For starters, we are both not very fond of parties. I am always bored at parties in clubs and you have never ever been to one as you are too scared to be sitting alone.'

'Hmm . . . this is true,' she agreed.

'You do not drink and I do not drink anymore,' I had been itching to tell her this.

'Really? Since when?' she said, with surprise.

'It has been a while . . . ' I replied, taking a sip of my coffee. It had no sugar in it and tasted good. 'Neither of us smoke and we have a limited number of close friends.' I was now counting the facts on my fingers and she looked amused trying to understand where I was headed.

'But we are so different, too,' she replied, and it was my turn to ask her why.

'I believe in destiny and your profile on Facebook says that you believe in no such thing,' she pointed out and I had nothing else to say on it, so I nodded. 'Agreed.'

'I believe everyone has a cosmic vibe and people with similar vibes attract each other, so because you and I are sitting here together after so many years, I do believe that we have similar vibes,' she said, cheering me up.

Later that evening, over our third cup of coffee, we discussed our love for books. She loved reading and I liked listening to audiobooks in my free time. Most importantly, both of us wanted to write a book based on our life at some point in our lives. 'I am yet to find my inspiration to write,' I told her, and then asked her why she had not pursued her love for writing further.

'I write or rather I should say that I scribble,' she smiled as she added.

'Have you sent your work to someone?' I was intrigued. I wanted to know more about it.

'No, not yet; it is so close to my heart that I want it to be perfect when I send it to a publisher,' she replied, shrugging her shoulders, sipping her coffee and then checking her watch.

I did notice that whenever she spoke about something which interested her a lot—something that she truly cares about and had a passion for—a flicker appeared in her eyes. They shone brightly for moments before a wet blanket was thrown over extinguishing the light. It was as if she was curbing her own feelings; some intense feelings that were trapped somewhere within her. In the little time that we had with each other to know one another better, I could sense that she at times tried to cover herself up with a personality that was not her own. She tried to be a distant version of herself; she wanted to come across as someone who she was not. Sometimes her true colours, or her true self struggled to come out but she was a pro at managing her emotional struggles. She was an amazing girl, and a perfect partner but she did not know it and I felt a deep urge to tell her how sensational and awe-inspiring she was.

'So tell me something. You say that you love reading and want to write a novel one day, then why haven't you started writing so far? I mean what are you waiting for?' she asked me, looking straight into my eyes, and before I could tell her why or even think of a suitable reason why I had not started working on anything, she hit me hard with her next statement which hurt me real bad.

'Sahil, you do not even have a full-time job for an excuse! If you have the passion and the skill, put it to use.' Somehow, I felt that she had purposely touched a nerve so that she would not be asked any more questions about her life. I had asked her about her relationship with her parents a while ago and that must have irked her. I was so lost in analyzing the flicker in her eyes and the change of her expressions that she caught me off guard with her question.

Unlike her, I am mostly quite straight-forward. 'I have always wanted to write a book, but never dared to start writing for I believed that if I started writing it and it didn't turn out to be good enough, then there would be nothing left to dream about. I will be like anyone else around here. I will not have this notion that I could be an amazing writer if I tried my hand at writing,' I tried to justify my actions or rather my lack of actions with some philosophy, but she was not going to buy it. 'Moreover, I have to get back one day and take care of my family's business,' I realized how important it was to appear to be in control and I was trying to show her just that. I wanted her to think of me as a sorted young man who had plans for his future. I wanted to come across as a person who had prospects as well as connections, but like always, she was not interested in my clichéd responses or what my social standing was as the son of Mr Malhotra.

'You want to know how I feel about what you just said?' she asked me, without really looking for an answer. If giving her an answer had been an option I would have said, 'No, I do not want to know,' as I knew her well enough by then to expect that she was going to punch me very hard and mercilessly with her words. But as I said, she was not looking for an answer. Before I could even nod, she added, 'I think you are too scared to write and you are just trying to find some lame excuses so that you do not have to face what you are so afraid of facing. You can find out if you are good at something only if you are brave enough to try it out—not by sitting on the idea and weaving a web of philosophy around it.'

'You do not know anything about all this. It is easy for you to say,' I said. I knew that I was acting like a child and that brushing aside her views was not going to change the fact that she was indeed right. But my actions did result in silence from her on the topic and she said no more. If she would have picked up anything around books to talk about again that evening, it would have ruined what had started blossoming between us. Not because she was wrong, but because I used to act like a kid about these things. I have worked on it a lot since then. Now, I am a better man, who can handle the truth better. I did learn that evening that the petite-looking girl Ayra was always too persistent for her tiny frame. When you first look at her, she looks passive. After that evening, I could bet my life that she was nothing close to being passive when she wanted to put a point across.

'It is in fact not at all easy for me,' she said. 'I work full-time. I am working on a children's book that I'm not sure will ever see the light of the day. I have this sudden eating disorder that doctors think is due to my rising stress levels. They want me to believe that it will go away on its own. My parents never wanted me to become a part of their lives and yet here I am beating all odds . . . ' Her voice went low and I knew that she was getting emotional talking about her life. I observed that she lowered her eyes trying to hide the pain behind the beautiful and happy persona, which she had created to deceive the world. Her words shook me out of not just my illusion of her, but also my own sleep. I was blessed to have a life as I did and what was I doing with it? I was trying to find new and innovative ways to run away from people who loved me. I am running away from everyone just to get rid of the responsibilities that I should have by then shouldered!

I wondered if I really did know anything about the real Ayra, her life, her family, her present situation. Did I really know anything at all about her? She looked very pale, in fact, she looked paler than when I had last seen her. Was it because of the eating disorder? She never mentioned all of this when we were chatting almost every day for the past many weeks. What did she mean by her parents never wanting her to be a part of their life? How can someone wish to disown their own child? There was so much to know about her that I felt sudden impatience growing in my heart. I was definitely seeing her in a different light and knew somewhere that knowing her better was going to make my feelings stronger for her. And there was no other way I wanted it to be. I resisted my urge to take her in my arms and tell her that she was much loved and that she was one of the strongest people I had ever met. She was definitely way better than me, and I wanted to ask her a million questions that were sprouting in my head at a lightning speed. She had tears in her eyes, but none spilled over as if they were showing off her resilience. Her will to take a stand for herself amazed me. The tears stayed in her eyes, not making their way down her cheeks and I felt tiny and childish compared to her. I was ashamed of my words and wanted to take them back, but words never come back. They do the damage and then make a home in the other person's memories. I prayed she would not rage against my words. And my prayers were answered. She was too good a person to hold grudges against people—people she loved and cared for.

A pure soul is rare and when you are around one, near one or are touched by one, you feel so good that it reflects in the surrounding. I felt the world disappear. She was no damsel in distress. She stood there like a woman who was capable of handling all that came her way. Ayra became my inspiration and her dreams became mine. She changed the topic and my questions were left lingering in the air. We then talked about movies. Shahid Kapoor was the one she was looking for and I envied him. Slowly as the sun went down and darkness started to envelop us to give us our space in the middle of the hustle and bustle, we started looking at each other for prolonged moments. After a while looking into each other's eyes, we were lost for some time only to come back to our physical surroundings when suddenly it started raining. The earthy smell of damp soil filled the void between us. Semi-drenched, we took shelter in the nearest shop and I gave her the scarlet silk scarf that I had bought from the store earlier that evening—my first ever present to her. 'Happy birthday!' I wished her again as she placed the scarf around her neck. It complimented her skin and she looked lovely. Yes, I did curse myself for not being able to give her the pair of earrings, which were waiting for us at the restaurant but this was no way less.

Like us, many other people pushed themselves under a tiny shelter and so she had to come closer to me. We spoke in whispers and marvelled at the rain. As the rain clouds started to disperse, people moved away and so did she. After around half an hour later, the rain finally stopped. It was time for us to part ways as I had to go to attend college the next day in another city and she had to get back home in time because that evening she was to be home alone. I offered to arrange a ride for her to go back home but she preferred to take an Uber instead after she dropped me at the airport.

'I hope I didn't hurt you,' she revisited the topic one last time as we were about to say goodbye to each other at the airport. There were so many people around going in and out of the place. I didn't want to go in; I wanted to talk to her all night that night but I knew that we both had to go. It was getting dark already and a sudden worry around her safety crept into my head.

'No!' I said shaking my head. I was amazed that she felt the way she did because if someone had to be sorry it had to be me. Meeting her that day and then going away made me realize that I did not want to go back. All this was so new to me—the meeting and the parting all happening at such short notice. I wanted to know her more and ask her everything that she had to tell me. I knew that it was all so sudden and also kind of rushed. But you cannot control your feelings—I felt embarrassed by my feelings despite being aware that they were as genuine as they can be. She had touched my heart with her genuineness and I smiled at her to tell her that it was all good—nothing that she ever said could have hurt me.

She gave me a warm smile in return and moved her tongue over her lips while she framed her thoughts into a sentence. In a grave, low voice—the kind that one uses with kids to make them understand very important matters of life—she told me, 'Sometimes I feel that intelligent people are so full of doubts nowadays while fools are full of themselves and overly confident. If intelligent people do not follow their dreams and only fools do, the world will be a circus for the next generation. Think about it.' With these words, she gently kissed my right cheek making me the happiest man at the airport at that time and murmured a soft goodbye. She walked away not looking back at me even once as I stood there almost melting under the cold breeze.

She was broken but pure magic. Her understanding of things made life so much simpler. Her presence was what I had been looking for in my life and by then I knew that as well.

When I reached home that night, I decided to work on my book as soon as I was done with the assignment from college. I will have to accept that I did struggle a lot trying to brush aside the memories of the gentle goodbye kiss, which took me by surprise. It was all happening very quickly and I wondered if I was living in some parallel universe. She was too good to be true and we had known each other for only a few weeks, yet it felt as if we had known one another for decades, and if you look at it, we really did. Her entry in my life made something click, like when a key clicks inside a lock and you know that you have found the right one.

'I hope she feels the same way about me,' I prayed. I'm someone who seldom prays but that evening called for a prayer to the Almighty in heaven. After I was done with a part of my assignment, I opened a new word document and started typing my thoughts into it. I was not letting the new-found inspiration and zeal go to waste.

By the way, the next day came with a surprise—a bouquet of sunflowers and a box of chocolates. There was a note stuck on the box of chocolates.

To You,
Thank you for the lovely evening. It was the best birthday ever for me. The sunflowers are to remind you that I like them the most, and next time get these for me, brat.
Enjoy your chocolates!
Ayra.

I still wonder how she managed to plan so many surprises, as I am a very poor planner of surprises. She was great, and that is why we were perfect for each other!

'I am going to put on weight if you keep sending me these.' I sent her a message on WhatsApp with the picture of her note and the chocolates.

CHAPTER 8

A few days later . . .

While I had managed to start writing this book about my life and my love for Ayra, I had lost all interest in studying, and completing my MBA appeared to be a mammoth task. I contemplated leaving the course and asking my father to let me be a part of the business. Ayra had made me see the world with the eyes of a mature man who need not prove anything to anyone but to himself. I realized that my happiness lies within me and I was determined to do what it takes to find happiness, because happiness won't find me. My happiness was to go back to my town, live with my parents, be with Ayra and do things professionally that made me dream big.

'What do you think?' I asked Ayra over a morning call a few days later. Our chats were now limited to the times when Ayra could take my call at home as her parents were suspicious about her frequent chatting and talking in a hushed voice in her room. I failed to understand what the fuss was all about, as she was a grown woman, and we were way past the infatuation phase. What I felt for her was pure love, but she didn't know about it, which was what was stopping me from talking to my parents or this was what I believed, as she never showed me that she was aware of my feelings. Her parents didn't really approve of any male friends that she had and I knew that convincing them for our marriage eventually would be a task. The good thing that had happened in the last week was that her parents had joined a yoga group in their society. This meant that she was alone at home from six to seven every morning and was available for a quick morning chat during which her voice sounded husky and sleepy.

'Is this what you truly want?' she asked me like she did a few times in the past whenever I told her that I missed being with my family and sooner or later I had to take over my dad's business.

'I truly want my family to be happy, and I want to write, too. I have written the first half of my initial draft, and I cannot wait for you to read it!' I told her excitedly.

'I don't think it is a good idea,' she told me upfront.

'What is not a good idea? You reading my work or me leaving my MBA?' I hoped that she was talking about the draft and not about the MBA.

'Me reading the first draft is not a good idea,' she clarified, 'I have known that you do not want to complete your MBA for a long time now. I never bought it up as I believed that you would talk about it sooner or later and here you are!' She never ceased to surprise me.

'Really? How? And why?' I probed a little.

'Because your heart is somewhere else,' she told me straightaway making no attempts to be polite.

'Yes it is,' I hope she was talking about herself, and about my family back home, of course, but mainly her. It was time that we addressed the elephant in the room, but how? That was all that I had to figure out.

Until I could do so, I decided to explain to her why I thought getting back home and starting work with Papa was a better decision. 'See, someday I do have to take over the business, it is my responsibility after all. And it is more stable . . . Like for the future when I get married,' I was pretty serious about what I was talking about and felt that I could steer the conversation in the right direction, but her giggle broke my confidence into pieces.

'What is it? What is so funny about all this?' I asked her sounding half as irritated as I really was.

'Nothing, I had not thought of the entire situation in that way,' she explained, 'Are you getting married? When? Who is the lucky gal?' she laughed louder than she usually did when at home. She was finding humour in my miseries.

'Not right now.'

'If you want to, then I do not mind though,' I had the urge to add.

'Then why worry right now?' She was right, why worry when I was not even sure if the girl that I had married in my dreams three times already was even in love with me or not. 'Hmmm . . . want to meet?' I asked her, and she agreed. I booked my third ticket to Delhi from Bengaluru in that week and in less than a few hours I was standing outside the airport in Bengaluru. I wondered what Papa would make of all this as all the flights were booked through his credit card, but I could handle that later. As explained initially, we are what one calls 'new money', which means that my parents still look at their credit card bills every month and circle any unusual spends. What worried me was why Papa had not blocked the card yet over suspicious transactions and why no one asked me about all these trips.

With a suspicion in my mind that my parents already knew about my frequent visits back home, which had nothing to do with them, I boarded the flight and a few hours later, found Ayra standing outside the Delhi airport, waiting for me. That day she had taken the first half-day off from work. 'How was your flight, Mr Frequent Flyer?' she asked me naughtily, and I grinned in response. 'Gooooood,' I told her, stretching the vowels.

'Where do you get all this money from to waste on flight tickets?' she inquired, and I decided to lie to her to make myself feel better.

'My mother wants to see her son very frequently and pays for the tickets.' I saw her expressions change. She didn't believe me, but there was no argument around the fact that my mother did love me a lot and wanted to see me more often than she did.

'I met her day before yesterday, and she was happier with you being away,' she said, sticking out her tongue in the same naughty way. I was glad that the two ladies had found company in each other and met often. Mummy often praised Ayra, even though Ayra hardly ever told me that she had met my mother. The only thing that my mother didn't like about Ayra was her dressing sense. 'She dresses too simple,' Mummy had mentioned a few times and I could see why. Ayra loved her cotton, while

Mummy was into all the designer stuff—new money does this to people, mostly.

Anyhow, that was not a big thing to worry about as I liked the way Ayra dressed up. She didn't like me spending money on her, and if I told her that I was spending my father's money just to date her, it would have embarrassed her further. So, a small white lie made it all good in her head. I was not completely lying on that occasion though. It was a Friday and I did have plans to stay over in Delhi for the weekend with my parents and cheer them up. They didn't need me for any cheering though, but I liked to think that they missed me as much as I missed them. A surprise visit to them was on my agenda.

After the series of bloopers on her birthday, I did learn that Ayra was a simple girl with simple needs and I need not show off to impress her. In fact, as she came from a humble background, I preferred to take her to places where she was comfortable having a conversation with me. I let her choose the venues, which were either cafes or fast-food restaurants. I was too happy being with her to care about the surroundings.

Since Ayra was working that day post noon, I proposed to drop her to her office after a quick breakfast at McDonald's. We reached a McDonald's near her office, and I ordered two 'Veg Breakfast Combos' for us. 'Coffee or coke?' a young boy standing behind the counter asked me. 'Coke for me and coffee for you, right?' I asked, looking at Ayra and noticing a sudden change of colour on her face. She looked ill; this was the first time I had seen her getting sick in front of me. I held her left hand, which was icy cold and sweaty.

'Are you alright, Ayra?' I was genuinely worried, for I had not seen her or anyone else turn so pale in my life. She nodded and then in a hurry, placed her work bag and a file on a random table and rushed into the washroom. I picked her bag and belongings and parked myself at a vacant table just outside the door, waiting for her. The staff at McDonald's had seen her run towards the loo and got our order at the table instead of calling out my name. I thanked him for his help and waited for her to appear again. She looked much better compared to when she had vanished into the washroom a while ago, but she was still looking unwell.

Was this the eating disorder that she had spoken about at Dilli Haat? Every time I wanted to know more about it, she brushed the topic under the carpet and raised another one instead. I didn't want her to feel awkward about it so I never really insisted on knowing it all as I didn't realize the intensity of it. At that moment, looking at her, I wanted to kick myself for not being persistent enough. She needed to see a doctor. I wanted to take her to one, but I didn't know if she would want to go. I didn't even know how to start a conversation about going to a hospital.

'What happened? Do you need anything?' I began by placing my hands on her shoulders.

'Nothing, just some acid reflux,' she said, shrugging her shoulders innocently and looking at all the food in front of us. Her brows arched—she couldn't eat it and neither could I.

'Will you be able to eat?' I asked her in a concerned tone, and as expected, she shook her head.

'No worries,' I said reassuringly and looked at her for a reaction. She said nothing. She seemed lost somewhere, closing her eyes every few seconds and breathing heavily. I had to know what was eating her, about her illness, and about her worries but that was not the right time. 'I will ask her tomorrow,' I made a mental note and started helping her pick up all her belongings in an attempt to take her outside the restaurant for some air. I gathered that she was looking to stay away from the smell of all that food, and I didn't want her to be sick again. So, I took her hand and signalled that we should make a move. 'The sooner she would be outside, the better she would feel,' I assumed.

'Hey! We can't leave all this food here,' she stopped midway and told me, pointing at the two trays of breakfast, which we had left untouched on the table behind us.

'What can we do?' I shrugged my shoulders, trying to comprehend what she meant.

Ayra walked up to the boy who was taking orders, and swiftly came back with two brown paper bags. I didn't want her to get sick again so I helped her pack the food on our table thinking that she wanted them for herself, but instead, she handed over the packets of food to the kids working as ragpickers who were playing outside the restaurant. She was the most thoughtful and caring person I ever knew.

I realized that she needed professional help and offered taking her to a doctor but she kept saying no. 'I have a doctor, and he has prescribed me some medicines. I forgot to take them in a hurry this morning and so this happened,' she said. I had no option but to agree with her. We did not go to the hospital. However, I did make her take her medicine right there in front of me. I also advised her to take a break from work that day and offered to drop her back home, but she was as stubborn as always. 'I have a few targets to meet this month and not everyone is as lucky as you are!' she said, mocking my position, and I gave her a weak smile. I knew that it was all wrong—she needed rest but she never listened to me when it came to her health.

Ten minutes later, Ayra took an auto to her office. In a hurry and with all the confusion due to her health, she had left her drawing book with me. It had fallen on the ground when she picked up her bag after she exited the washroom, and I picked it up. It was a heavy binder book with numerous pages in it, and I had held onto it as it made more sense that I carried it and not her. I did not know at that time what the notebook carried and assumed it was related to her work and the targets that she was referring to. Immediately, while still standing at the same place, which was the last step at the mall where I had bid her goodbye, I dialled her number to tell her that I had her notebook because the last thing that I wanted was for her to panic when she found it missing.

I waited for her to answer the call, unaware that what I had in my hand that morning was going to change everything I knew about her.

'Is it important? I can bring it to you if you want,' I proposed, as that would have given me another chance to meet her that day.

'Of course, it is important! It has the illustrations for my children's storybook,' she told me, 'I do not need it today though.'

'Oh okay,' I was sad because we were not going to meet again then. 'I can drop it off to your office if you want me to?' I told her. I hoped she would say yes and I really wanted to as she was okay now.

'Don't stress over it my brat. I will take it from you tomorrow if that is okay?' she suggested in a low voice, and I happily agreed, for this was the first time she had referred to me as being 'hers'. Also, from that day on, she called me 'her brat' and I didn't mind being it. Soon, she reached her office and disconnected the call. I forgot to ask her if she was feeling any better, so I texted her instead. Floating in the clouds of love, intoxicated with happiness and filled with hope, I stretched my right arm to signal an auto. One came up to me in no time and I was on my way to meeting my parents and relishing some homemade food.

'I am good, but please do not open the book. Promise me you won't', a message beeped on my phone in less than a minute after I reached home.

'I won't promise' is what I intended to type, but instead, I typed the following—'I won't, promise.' A misplaced comma hurt no one.

Till then, I had no interest in the plain-looking orange notebook that lay on my study table, but as soon as I read her message, curiosity sprung into my heart, and all I wanted to do was to open and see what was inside. She had mentioned that there were illustrations and who doesn't like looking at some drawings?

I wanted to know more about her dream project, especially because she wanted to keep it a secret.

Later that day . . .

My parents were more than thrilled to meet me after what they referred to as 'ages'. It had only been a few days since I was back in Delhi, but since I'd been flying back and forth for my dates with Ayra, we were going to spend a weekend together after a long time. At times, I did feel bad about keeping my visits to the city a secret. Then, many months later, my parents told me that they had been aware all along that I had been sneaking in and out of Delhi without meeting or informing them—after all, they were my parents and I was using my father's card to book all the tickets. Then the guilt had turned into sheer embarrassment.

Anyhow, coming to that day, Mummy had prepared my favourite meal—Daal Chawal and *Bharta*. All the while I ate, she kept pointing out how her only child was 'going thinner and skinnier every minute'—her words, not mine. Her starving child attacked the tasty looking food like a hungry gorilla and soon was burping and taking an antacid for impending acid reflux.

'I have always told you to eat slowly and to chew well,' my mother chided me, never leaving out any opportunity to impart her little medicinal knowledge. 'How do you even manage without us in that city is what I wonder at times!' she added with a hint of mirth, and I smiled a fake smile to hint that she should stop making fun of me for the day.

'How is your MBA?' Papa asked, looking up from his laptop. My homecoming that day was one of the rare occasions when I witnessed him working from home as he detested taking time off from his office.

'It is going okay,' I said, wondering how to start a conversation related to my plans of quitting the MBA.

I had almost fought over this one and now to go back and tell them that they were right, and I was not was going to be tough. But it had to be done—the sooner the better. So I carefully began. 'Why are you working from home, Papa? Have you not been keeping well?' I asked him and he gave me a sarcastic smile—he knew that I was onto something.

'I have been perfectly fine. I had promised your mother that I shall be spending more time with her once you have flown out of our nest. I work from home three days a month now that you finally have made your way out,' he said with a wink. He was grinning when he asked, 'Why do you ask?'

'No, nothing. I was thinking that as you guys are moving on in your life now, maybe I should be around here more and take up some responsibilities like an adult. I was, in fact, thinking of dropping the idea of this MBA to help you out with the business. I know the MBA would be an added advantage, but then everyone is an MBA nowadays, so maybe we can hire one,' I blurted it all out in one go, sitting down next to my father and not looking at anyone in the eye. A deadly silence followed, which was interrupted by the doorbell. One of the servants went out to open the door, and my mother was summoned. She left the room without saying a word. I was really counting on her support. Now it was only Papa and me, sitting in the dreaded silence. Coming back home was proving to be harder than leaving.

'Is everything okay at college?' Papa finally broke the chilling silence, and I had to look at him.

'Yes, all is good there. I just miss you guys and being away made me realize how I have been running away from my responsibilities for years,' I stated the truth, or rather the partial truth to be specific. I had not told him how coping up with studies was getting hard or that I wanted to be a writer or that a girl was taking up most of my time every day and I wanted to get married to her and start a life as a married man in love.

Papa didn't ask anything either; instead, he looked at me trying to search through my soul. He knew that I had frequently been travelling to Delhi without telling them and was probably waiting for me to come out clean. Soon, Papa resumed his work and Mummy started asking me random questions like what I wanted for dinner or if I needed anything to be packed to take back to Bengaluru—they were sending me back!

Tired after an eventful first half of the day, I decided to retire into my bedroom and muster up some courage so that I could have a conversation about my future again before I left. Both my parents had their day charted out; neither of them seemed to mind my absence, and as a single child that did hurt.

However, with a stomach full of food, it was hard to concentrate on anything else, so I took a much-needed nap and when I woke up a few hours later, I was alone. Both my parents had left to fulfil a social engagement that evening. With nothing else to do and no one around to pester, I decided to take a quick peek into Ayra's book. I wanted to know what her dream project was all about. She had mentioned that the book had her drawings and illustrations. I had a feeling that Ayra was a talented artist so I had to see her work. Her being so shy about everything related to this book was very surprising for me and it made me more curious than ever. So, that was the right time and opportunity to check the book out without her knowledge. I moved back into my room and bolted the door; there was no one at home apart from a servant and I knew that even if he walked on me looking at Ayra's drawing book, he would not think of it as anything wrong. But when you know that you are doing something that you should not be doing, your mind starts directing your body to take precautionary steps—that was exactly what I was doing there. I was being mindful that no one catches me.

I drew the curtains, switched on the lights at my desk and stared at the book. It was a little worn out at the edges. I turned a leaf over—the first page had her name written in calligraphy. Her handwriting was beautiful, and even though I am no expert in handwriting and calligraphy, I could tell that she was fairly good at what she did. I traced my fingers over her name. I visualized her sitting alone at her desk someday, when this book would have been brand new, and writing her name on it, making it her own with her hand delicately holding a black pencil. I imagined her moving the pencil across the paper making markings that would stay there. It was so easy for me to picture her even with my eyes wide open. Her face was almost always there in my head, ready to pop up in my imagination.

Then there was a sudden commotion outside my room. It was our clumsy househelp who dropped something like he always did, but my heart had come into my mouth and I realized that I was panting for no reason. 'Why am I so scared? It is just a book. I am not going to commit a murder,' I told my racing heart. 'Let us get this done with,' I said to myself out loud.

On the next page were a few sketches of a lioness from different angles—the face and just the eye were drawn in the corner. As I kept turning the pages, one after the other, a story started to unfold. It was about a lioness and a jackal who tricked the lioness many times. She had very carefully and neatly drawn the scenes and written a few lines about the scene on every page. Some of the illustrations were coloured with pencil colours while most were drawn using a standard grey pencil. Like a child, I marvelled at each and every page and wondered for how long she had been working on it. She was not kidding about her passion, and her love for her book was way stronger than what I had for mine. She must have given years' worth of thought while preparing the story and describing the scenes. Amazed and awed, I reached the end of the story, which was not the end of the storybook—a few more followed, and they held the reason why she had made me promise not to open the book. It was a note, or more of a brief memoir.

My first memory of you is from a hot summer day. I loathed your presence in the house, but my parents loved to have you over. You used to bring those video cassettes which contained movies about fast cars over in your loud cars that had even louder music in them, and watched those movies with my father. I hated being forced to stay in the same room as you. I was seven years old then or maybe younger. You used to bring your younger sister, who was my elder sister's best friend, with you. We were all cousins but little did you care. While our sisters played with their dolls in the other room, my parents forced me to sit with you. You used to make me sit on your lap and touch me when no one was watching. You used to kiss me, declaring how cute my cheeks were while your hands made me uncomfortable at other places.

I remember my parents telling how much 'bhaiya' loves spending time with me and how rude I was to have bitten you the last time you were babysitting me. I ran into the other room sobbing, but my mother didn't care. She told you that I was just a shy little girl who lacked social skills. 'She will improve,' she declared, loud enough for me to hear. They never understood why I cried looking at you or why I shivered whenever a new male relative walked through the front door. They blamed it all on my confidence level. They thought of me as a mere child who did not even know how the world works. This was primarily because they did not want me to. All they cared about was you. They didn't want to lose the babysitter who was always at their beck and call.

That evening too they had to go to a wedding, and you and your sister were to stay with us. I begged my mother to take me along. 'I will be good, Mummy, I will behave well,' I remember telling her. 'Stay at home and be nice to bhaiya and didi,' she said, glaring at me with her big eyes, knowing very well that this would shush me.

'Bhaiya', there was nothing brotherly about you. No brother does that to his sister. My heart thumped faster as I saw my parents leave on the grey scooter and I ran into my parents' room before you had the opportunity to lock the door and hold me. I hid behind the curtains hoping that you would get back to watching your movie if you won't find me standing behind you. But you did not. You called out my name a few times knowing very well where I was and finally took the curtain away, exposing me. I screamed to alarm my sister who was too engrossed in her games to notice. You tried to

pick me up, and when I kicked you in your stomach, you dragged me into the storeroom by my hair, laughing your evil laugh, while trying to cover my cries.

In the dark storeroom, as you closed the door, I knew what was to happen for you had done it to me before. I fought your fondling hands as much as I could and almost puked on you when you forced me to open my mouth. It had happened in the past, too—everything else is a blurred memory like a box that my mind has purposefully sealed, so that I can never access the images and pain hidden in it.

When my parents came back home, I crawled out from under their bed. You had threatened me not to say a word but I had to—it was my only escape route. I walked up to my mother, who was taking off her gold jewellery and sitting in front of her dresser. 'Mummy, bhaiya is bad,' I told her, not knowing how to tell her the rest or what exactly to say to her for I did not know the exact term myself. 'Why, did he scold you?' she asked me, not taking her eyes off from her reflection in the mirror. I know now what I should have said, but at that time, all I could manage to say was, 'He touched me and made me cry.' As soon as I told her this, I started sobbing. 'You must have not behaved well; he told me that he had to squeeze your arm when you were not eating,' my mother told me, unmoved by my words, and it took me by surprise.

She looked exhausted and was in no mood to listen to a child, who would have sounded half asleep. So, she shooed me away, and I obeyed, like always. The next day, before going to school, I tried again to explain it to her. 'He is bad, he dragged me,' I told her, as she packed my lunch, barely listening.

Then, again when I came back home, I picked up the topic; this time, my father was in the same room as well. 'He locked me in the store,' I told them while crying.

'Were you alone? Did you get scared? Did he hit you? I shall talk to him,' my concerned father told my mother and me.

'Were you alone in the darkroom?' my mother patiently asked me—this time, looking at me straight in the eyes. 'No, he was with me in there,' I told her.

'They are finally taking me seriously! Thank god!' I thought.

'She is again making up stories—last night, she told me that he made her cry; in the morning, she said that he dragged her, and now, it's the storeroom. You know her; she likes making up stories. Don't you remember how she made up the story around that missing pencil and then the pencil was found under her bed, and then her stories about that mad dog . . . ?' my mother told him, and both of them laughed at the stories which I had made up in my head in the past and like that, the discussion was over.

I might have made up a story about a mad dog or a missing pencil, but which child doesn't do that to get away from trouble—I was, after all, a child. But I knew that I couldn't explain it to them.

The next time you and your sister were at our house, I knew you would do the same thing, and I also knew that my parents wouldn't believe me. I knew that fighting you would mean more pain and tears, so I gave in so that you would leave me alone. This went on and on, and I cried many silent nights braving you with tearful eyes every time I was alone with you. You never cared, for you never saw me as a child, who was younger than your own kid sister. You never cared for my pain or the scars that you left on my childhood. I never wish to go back in time like all kids do, for I know that my past has a monster in it.

I was grateful to God when you got through that engineering college; in fact, I was happier than you were. I was finally free from *you but not from the memories that you gave me. They haunt me night after night. Tonight, too, I woke up bathed in my own sweat, fighting you off in my dream only to realize that much time has passed.*

No matter how much time passes by, I will always hate you, for you spoiled my childhood for me.

After so many years, you came back to haunt me in my dreams, but I won't let you do that. Not anymore—I will face my fears now.

I was perspiring as if I had lived the moments she described in her note. By the time I was done reading, my hands had started trembling. I wondered if it was fiction, or a part of her life that she wished to hide under the pages of a children's book. Looking at the way she described everything, I had no reason to not believe that it was all a part of her past. I didn't know what to do and how to talk about it all with her; I didn't even know if I actually wanted to talk about it. Her mood swings, her reluctance to share her mobile number, her eating disorder—all of it suddenly made sense to me.

I had broken the promise I made to her, and now I knew something about her that changed everything. I was shocked, to say the least, and my heart felt as if it was beating out of my body.

CHAPTER 9

I was shocked, to say the least. The words that I had just read made my world spin. I had seen all of this in movies, had read so many horrific deeds in newspapers, but I had never really thought that someone I knew and loved, could have been a victim. I also knew that it was wrong on my part to break her trust, but I had done it, and now there was no way to undo it. I had looked into the most intimate part of her heart and there was no way that I could just forget what I had read and pretended that I knew nothing about it.

I was the culprit, but the same crime of mine had made me see Ayra is a light that never fell on her otherwise. My view of her changed. I understood her better and could find a correlation between her past and her present. I understood, if not completely, then to some extent, why she burst into sudden tears at times, and why she was a different person one moment and someone else a moment later. I understood her sudden shivers and her hesitance to share her phone number. I understood her lack of trust in men. I even understood her laughter that was a cover for all the pain underneath. I understood the brightness that covered the darkness. While I did understand all of it, I was at a complete loss of words as well as reactions.

I was scared to talk to her about it, without making her angry or without losing her. The judgement of right and wrong leaves you when you are encountered by truth so naked. The society never ceases to amaze you with examples that make one question the entire system altogether. I couldn't shake the images from my head of the child who had experienced it all because I knew the child. I knew her around the time that it was going on and that killed me, because she did try to seek help from me as well. In a few words she had described the demon who tormented her in her stories during lunch time. She at times had even spoken about her nightmares but I too was only a child and could not comprehend her cries for help which were disguised as stories. Her parents' attitude amazed me, because even as a child, I knew that she was not lying, I knew that there was something wrong but I couldn't place a finger on what it was. Before I spoke to Ayra and told her that I had read her note, I had to talk to someone, but I didn't want to share intimate details of her life with just a random person, as that would be wrong as well. I needed to talk to someone whom I could trust. I needed to speak to someone who would understand.

I knew that I was in love with this broken girl—I had always been—but the realization of how deep my feelings were for her had only sunk in recently. She made me see things like no one else did; she inspired me to follow my dreams; she believed in them more than I did myself, and she made me feel so much better. She made me aspire to be a better version of myself. So, if knowing her past had done anything to my feelings for her, it was to deepen them into my soul and carve her name there for eternity. She was the epitome of strength, courage, and love that I was fortunate to have known and been in love with. What I was struggling with was my ability to deal with the situation and tell her that I knew of her past. I was born in a perfect family and am blessed to have parents who dote on me. I needed advice and help from a person, who would have seen or faced a similar situation in their lives, and so, I turned to my best friend Bhanu and his partner Pathak. Well, Pathak is his surname as he wishes to be addressed by his surname only. Bhanu, on the other hand, detests his surname and is known as Bhanu by all. He even tried to change his name on his passport more than once, only to be stopped from doing so by Pathak.

My best friends from my tuition classes, Bhanu and his partner Pathak, know each other from the time when they used to poop in their diapers, literally. Their fathers were best friends from college, who married their girlfriends, who were neighbours. They did everything together, from school to tuitions, to summer vacations and holiday trips. The boys were thick as thieves while growing up, just like their fathers, even though both Bhanu and Pathak were stark opposites of each other and still are.

Bhanu is an outgoing musician who loves to party and host people at his home, while Pathak is an introverted

call centre manager, who likes to stay alone and read books.
Bhanu took Arts in college while Pathak was a commerce
student. Bhanu dresses up in cool and funky clothes of all
sorts and is very fashion-conscious, while Pathak is usually
either seen in formal attire or a relaxed pair of jeans and plain
t-shirts. One day, the two boys met after college for a walk
in the park and for drinks, which they occasionally shared,
away from the eyes of their families. After a few drinks, the
conversation steered towards life and other serious things.
Even after walking and talking for a few hours, when they
couldn't bring themselves to close their conversation, they
decided to get food and drink some more beer. Two more
beers and endless arguments later, they realized how much
they loved each other, but both of them were scared to
tell the other as they didn't really know how the other
felt about it all. For all they knew, it was a taboo to even
think about it. But they could not contain it for long. So,
after one more beer, the truth came out, first from Bhanu's
mouth. Despite all dissimilarities, Bhanu and Pathak fell in
love with each other.

Their families didn't know till much later that the boys
had found love in each other, and when they did, they didn't
take it well. They broke all ties with them after a series of
traumatic attempts to tear them apart. Bhanu, the rebel, didn't
care much for his family, because they didn't accept him for
who he was but shamed him for his life choices. His father
called him names and that was the end of it for Bhanu—he
packed his bags and left his home to pick Pathak up. He had
it enough. Regardless of what had happened, Pathak was still
heartbroken and wanted to reconcile with both the families.

After being thrown out of their homes in Delhi, Pathak found a job in Bengaluru, and both of them moved to the city. They have been their happiest since the move, and I was happy for them. It was time that I approached them for some advice. They had seen more of life than I had; they were more experienced, and I knew that I could trust them to keep my secret safe with them.

When I called their landline, Bhanu and Pathak were arguing about a piece of furniture for their new home. The call was answered by their maid, who put me on speakerphone, so that I could talk to both of them at the same time. I listened quietly as Pathak explained to me why turquoise matched with the colour scheme of their home as opposed to orange, and why I should help him convince Bhanu to change his mind.

'I need to talk about something much more important than this, guys!' I couldn't really talk or think about anything other than Ayra at that moment.

A sudden halt in noises made me check if they had hung up on me. They were there, waiting for me to talk—both Bhanu and Pathak were all ears. I was ashamed of confessing that I read Ayra's book and begged them to help me speak to her.

'We live in a society where we are labelled, and these labels form your identity,' Bhanu began talking, and I sat down on my bed to listen to him. 'So, when I told my parents that I had decided to go against the label that the world had put on me, they didn't take it well because they couldn't think of this whole situation as a matter of "fact", but decided to look at it as a matter of "choice".

They initially thought that they could change my choice or lure me into choosing what was right for me as per them or rather as per the society. "There is no right," is what I told them and that is when they broke all ties with me.' His voice had pain in it. I had known him for years and I was aware that somewhere inside the tough exterior, the 'I do not care' Bhanu was a sweet and innocent child, who longed for his parents' acceptance. I had never thought that I would ever hear the pain in his voice as he was always the happy one. He pretended to be the stronger one in the pair and acted as if he was the one who didn't care, but I knew that he did care. His heart was in Delhi with his family; he just did not show that he was still waiting for that one phone call.

'She is a girl, labelled to be "quiet" and to "bear it all". She has lived through hell, and when she tried to tell her closest people, who she expected to stand up for her, they chose to ignore her and then label her as a liar. She must be all broken inside. Her ability to trust someone would be really low and when you tell her that you read her book, even when she had categorically asked you not to, and that you have broken her trust so early on in your relationship, she will react. Expect a lot of reaction from her,' Pathak added.

'React as in? Get angry?' I had to be prepared for what was coming my way. Anger was something that I was prepared for, and a lot of shouting, too. I kind of knew that she would react. I would have done so, too. It was only natural.

'Yes, she will be angry, like she would have been when the thing happened to her. She might try to take out her anger and all the built-in frustration on you by screaming at you, and by getting angry and calling you names. In the worst case, she might just shut herself down. No one can predict. But you must let her react the way she chooses to. Also, initially, after my parents told me that there was something wrong with me, I kind of believed it for a while. She might also be in that frame of mind because she got no help from anywhere. She might be thinking that somewhere it was all her fault. Society does a good job of victim-blaming and shaming in most cases. You need to tell her how it isn't her fault and you need to tell her that you love her no matter what,' Bhanu added.

'But I have not yet told her that I love her; I do not know if I do love her, actually,' I do not know why I said that last line.

'Why are you calling up then? I know that you love her and you do, too. It is time that you tell her.' He caught my lie outright and once more, I realized that I am not even half as mysterious as I believe myself to be.

I bid them goodbye, knowing very well that they would have resumed their argument around home decor as soon as the call was disconnected. I had a lot of thinking to do. Before hanging up, I made them promise that they will never bring this up, ever in front of anyone. I trusted them, even though only moments ago, I had broken Ayra's trust.

The next day, Ayra messaged me that she could meet me in the evening. It was a Saturday, and she was off work. Because her parents didn't like her going out to meet boys, she had come out of her house on the pretext of meeting a girlfriend from college. She had to be back home before the sunset—this was the first thing she told me as soon as we met again at the same place: Dilli Haat. I wanted her to remember our outing together on her birthday before I told her about her drawing book. I could have kept the truth from her and not told her anything about it as it had not made any difference to my love for her. If anything, my feelings had become stronger for her and I wanted to protect and love her all her life, and all my life. But keeping the secret from Ayra wouldn't have been right on my part, so I had to tell her.

We decided to meet at two in the afternoon. It was a sunny day. I reached on time, and so did she. Right at 2 p.m., I saw her walk into the security door, dressed in a long flowing peach-coloured dress. She carried a big white handbag and approached me with a hesitant smile. I looked back at her nervously with a big bouquet of flowers in my hand. This time, I had got her sunflowers, which were her favourite, with a lone red rose, to remind her of me. I wanted to make a good impression that day. It was still a date.

'Hi,' she said, looking at the flowers. 'You finally remembered?' she joked and I smiled back at her, hoping that I would manage to tell her how much I loved her before she called me a 'stupid brat' again and disappeared like she did in school.

'Yes, I did. These are for you,' I told her, stretching my left hand to extend the bouquet for her to hold it.

'Thanks,' she said, which was an expected response from her. She smiled at the flowers and then back at me.

'That rose in there is me saying "hi", sitting prettily amongst your favourite flowers,' I told her, pointing out the rose and she laughed, though I noticed she was looking a bit tense. She might have known that I was not one of the people who could keep their hands off other people's things and secrets.

I was nervous that I was going to break her heart, and that was going to shatter mine into pieces too, but I had to tell her. Maybe I was making a mountain out of a molehill, but I had to find out; I had to come out clean. We walked along the lanes self-absorbed for a while; she wanted me to talk and I was too scared to talk about what I had in my mind. After a few moments of silence, I finally started the small talk and gradually built a conversation around our first meeting at the same place a few weeks ago.

Looking at all the shops, I carefully made her recall our time together when we were last there; when I had a different thing on my mind, and when I was looking at her in a different light altogether. I pointed out the places where we had enjoyed our time together the most. As we reached the place where I had purchased a gift for her, I asked her to halt and presented her with a pair of anklets. She refused to accept gifts—she always did—so I had to actually try all the filmy tactics for her to accept it. 'My Papa will not like it, and what will I tell Mummy?' she kept repeating, as I begged her not to make me take it back. She was worried about her parents' opinion the most, but I made her wear them, post a round of emotional blackmailing, of course. The moment she said 'okay' in a low voice, I dropped to one knee. She gasped as I sat down on the ground in front of everyone and hooked the first one around her left ankle. 'I will wear the other one on my own . . . ' she whispered, squatting next to me. I handed over the anklet, and she wore it delicately. As she hooked it around, I whispered the precious three words into her ears, 'I love you.' I had been holding on to them for a while and felt a sudden relief as soon as they were out there in the open for her to respond to.

I wanted to know how she felt about me before I told her about the trust-breaking act of mine. She raised her head and faced me with her big almond-shaped eyes wide open under her black-rimmed spectacles. I lifted the back rimmed glasses off her face, and she blinked a few times to adjust her vision. At this moment, I was not sure if she had actually heard me the first time I had confessed my feelings, so I decided to repeat what I had said a few moments ago, just in case. 'I love you,' I said, breathing heavily into her face that was so close to mine that I could smell her minty breath. She smiled and bit her lower lip, and just then, the rain gods decided to interfere, again.

'Why, god, why?' I muttered under my breath. Our trip to this place was jinxed as every time we came to the place, it rained.

I held her hand as we rushed, looking for shelter from the rains, like tens and hundreds of people around us. As we headed into a tea stall, countless raindrops fell on our heads, drenching us. 'My drawing book!' she exclaimed, looking at it as I held it in my hand. The corners of the book were a little wet by then. Panting, I told her that it did not look too bad. 'But my illustrations are all done in colours—they will bleed and ruin everything,' she told me worriedly and informed me that the 'jackal' has too many details on it to be done again. She looked so concerned about her drawing going bad that without thinking much, the next few words just slipped out of my mouth involuntarily.

'I know. You have sketched them all so beautifully. But they will be alright, I guess. Don't worry,' I tried to calm her down, forgetting how ill-timed my words were!

Ayra looked at me with such a broken expression that it cannot be described in words. I felt so small and so wrong at that moment that I wished the earth would open up and swallow me before she cried. I anticipated a flow of emotions that would take me down with it. I expected her to scream or shout or scold me, but none of it happened. I had expected her to react violently, but she didn't. Instead, she fixed her eyes on the ground and ignored my being there as if I was not present at the scene anymore. I decided to do the right thing, so I pleaded guilty and begged her to say something. 'I cannot tell you that I understand how you feel as I do not. All I can tell you is that talking helps, so talk to me. I love you more than I have loved anyone. Please do not go all quiet on me. Say something, please!' But she had withdrawn into herself; she had shut out the world and me.

Sometimes, when you need the outside world to disappear, you run from it; you find a hiding place within and like a snail, you just curl. The world ceases to exist, and that is what Ayra had done.

'Talk to me please . . . ' I whispered into her ear many times, but there was no reaction from her. I had a strong urge to hold her tight and tell her that I was there for her no matter what had happened in the past. I wanted to hug her and tell her that she could trust me. There were so many eyes on us already as I was forcing a girl, who stood looking at nothing in particular, to talk. People must have assumed that I was probably harassing her. I wanted to embrace her, but I did not do so as it would have been inappropriate. With so many eyes on us, the last thing which I wanted was to make a scene at the place. Not a single drop of tear came out of her eyes. It was as if her tears for that part of her life had gone dry; as if she had cried all that she could for what happened then in her life and now all that was left were scars so deep that they would only bleed if they were touched again.

Slowly, the rain stopped, and she walked away from me, leaving her drawing book with me as a sign of betrayal to haunt me every night. The sunflowers lay on the ground rejected. I did have the satisfaction of telling her that I loved her, and despite her not telling me that she loved me too, I felt that she did, and later on, she said it, too. But at that moment, I wondered if my words had changed anything about how she felt about me. The least that I could expect was hatred, for any emotion was better than her being so distant like the way she had left me alone, standing at the tea stall.

I went back home that evening and took a flight back to Bengaluru to resume my course, which I had the least interest in completing.

The Present
August 2018

The alarm was in place, which meant that her nurse had left the house. I slowly opened the door as I knew that she would have been sleeping by then. Ayra's nurse,

Samita, usually messaged me whenever she left for the day in my absence, but she had forgotten to do so that evening. A new medicine was introduced to Ayra a few days ago, and she had been responding well. The only thing that I didn't really like about it was that she slept a lot because of the new drugs. 'She needs as much rest as she can get for the medicine to work properly,' her doctor had told me. He had very high hopes for the new drugs as the success rate was quite high in young patients who responded positively to the medicine. For Ayra, it was still in the trial phase. I felt his positivity run through me, too—every time I gave her the dose, I believed that she was getting better; she looked more relaxed and less in pain as well. I probed her to check if she was indeed feeling better or if it was just me going crazy. And every time I asked her, she stuck her tongue out and closed her eyes like a child, mocking me.

The lights had been dimmed, so I tiptoed into the living room and placed my things at the table in the hallway that lead to our bedroom. Mummy and Papa had gone to the Vaishno Devi temple in Jammu to pray for Ayra, while she had insisted me to attend the house-warming party thrown by Bhanu and Pathak. I didn't want to wake her up, so I quietly bolted the door of the bedroom and went into the study to take out her files to prepare for our visit to the hospital the next day.

I peeped through our bedroom door before closing it. There she was, sleeping soundly like a child, most likely dreaming of stars. She loved stars and everything about the night.

My parents had grown very fond of this lovely girl, who was least bothered about us because she was slowly inching towards leaving us all.

'Keep her happy,' Papa had instructed me, when he was leaving for Jammu that morning.

'I am trying,' I told him, and broke down for the first time in my adult life in front of my parents. I was upset because our life was not going as per my plans, and there was nothing that I could do about it. I wanted to see the world with her but there she was, lying in bed, unwell. There was always a nurse at duty, which meant we hardly spoke to each other in privacy and we spent most of our days at hospitals.

'Not everything goes as per the plan, my brat. Sometimes, we need to work as per someone else's plan. This is all as per the plan—not yours, but God's. Trust your journey in the world, trust your fate, your destiny and trust mine, too,' she used to say calmly, and I wondered why and how. She was the one suffering and she was the one who was not complaining, at all.

I wanted Ayra to be very happy for as long as she lived. I had seen her in so much pain already that now all I wanted for her was peace and happiness. One thing that would really make her happy was to see my book being published as soon as possible, for our time together was limited. A publishing house was interested in publishing my book only if I could finish writing it on time. In the recent past, I had been struggling with the book as words failed me. I was so lost and preoccupied with my thoughts about Ayra that writing had to take a back seat. It had been a few days since I started wondering if I could really make this wish of hers come true. She always read me like a book, and no matter how much I tried to conceal my troubles from her, she looked through me to find them.

As I made my way to the bed to join her, I found a note on my pillow on my side of the bed, on which was kept the anklet that I gave her when I told her that I loved her for the first time at Dilli Haat.

To You,

I saw you struggle with your manuscript last night. I saw you tear the pages off of your diary in despair. You are trying something new, something that you had always wanted to do but never really did. I am no expert at writing books but I am an expert now at trying new things even when I know that they might not really work.

I have a piece of advice for you: please be patient with yourself and give yourself time to grow. Think about how proud your past self shall be if he could see you now.

Rome was not built in a day, remember?

Life opens up new gates of opportunities for you—either you take a step and walk towards them, or you stay afraid of crossing over. You have an opportunity that so many people will die for, so make the most of it, but do not be unkind to yourself while you do so.

After you have read this, come into the bed and snuggle with me.

With Love.

After reading her note, I knew that I had to continue writing our story no matter how much it pained me to revisit it all. So, I tucked the note between my fingers and walked into the study. It was time to start writing again . . .

CHAPTER 10

Ayra did block me from all her social media accounts as well as on WhatsApp. This lasted for a day and then I found myself unblocked again. Maybe she thought of what had happened and decided that she was being too harsh. I do not know exactly what caused this blocking and unblocking as we never really spoke about it again. I knew that the situation was not normal, her past was not normal, what she had lived through and what she had endured was not easy to forget, but I really wanted to talk to her to clear the air. While I was not barred from any of her accounts, there was no interaction between us for a week and I was failing at concentrating on my studies as well as everything else. I knew that she was being real mature by not screaming at me or calling me names but her silence hurt equally. Every time I found her online, I wanted to call her or text her, but I was too scared of being rejected. Sometimes, humans think too much and we tend to feel very little; we tend to empathize very little and understand very little. This is what the main problem is in relationships. I didn't want to do so—I wanted to feel her pain; I wanted her to feel my happiness and I wanted us to feel the love that we had for each other. But all of this could happen only if we spoke to each other and spoke about 'us'.

It took me a week to gather enough courage to call her again from a PCO as I did not really want her to disconnect my call even before I could get the chance to hear her voice.

'Hello,' she answered my call, and I began my rehearsed speech.

'I am sorry for what I did. I should not have opened the journal. I should have respected your privacy,' I paused for her to either hang up or say something. She did neither of the two, which was a good sign, so I continued, 'Can we talk about it, please?'

Her father called her that very moment, and she disconnected the call with a 'bye'.

Fifteen minutes later, she dropped in a message on WhatsApp. She was going to call me again, from a friend's house in another half an hour. That half an hour was the longest half an hour of my life. Minutes passed like hours, and finally, she called.

'Hi,' she sounded low.

'Hi, how have you been?' I am not very good at small talk.

'Good, listen, about that day. I had to . . . I mean . . . I am sorry . . . ' she said

'Sorry? Why? I am sorry to have invaded your personal space,' I quickly corrected the situation. She had nothing to be sorry about.

'Okay,' she said, lost in her thoughts.

'Are we okay, then?' See, I am terrible at small talk, or any talk in general.

'No,' she took me by surprise with her answer.

I didn't say anything. I wanted her to tell me whatever she wanted to say as I wanted her to talk. She could speak to me about everything. After a small period of silence, she did talk.

'I know you have read something and would have questions about it,' she told me.

'No, I do not want to ask you anything. All I want to tell you is that I love you, a lot,' I confessed once again. 'Do you love me? I want to get married to you,' I said. I never expected to propose to her over a call, but there I was, not bent on one knee and yet proposing to the girl I loved with all the sincerity I could muster up, across the phone line.

'You need to know some things before I respond to your proposal,' she told me calmly and then exhaled as if she had a huge burden to unburden.

'Nothing can change my feelings for you,' I was sure of that.

'I was three years old when my mother died. I was getting over the grief when the police found my father to be the main suspect and took him away. He did indeed plan her murder. I was left in the custody of my father's sister and her husband, whom I call Mummy and Daddy now. My father is now married to some other woman.' Her words hit me like a rocket. I believed that there was nothing about her that would change anything, but this truth, this revelation, meant that I had to talk to my parents before I could promise marriage to Ayra.

I said nothing. I could hear her breathing slow down and after a few moments, she disconnected the call saying that I could take my time and come back to her if I wanted to. Her answer to my question was 'yes' and that she did love me, too. I wanted her to tell me that she loved me; I wanted her to say yes to becoming my wife, but what I had never anticipated was the extent to which her past was messed up.

I called my mother instantly and told her that I was in a situation. I told her about Ayra's father and her deceased mother and asked her for her approval. 'I love her a lot, Mummy, and I want you and Papa to be happy about this marriage,' I told her truthfully.

'She had told me all about her father and mother on the day I had first met her,' my mother told me, taking me by surprise. She was okay with it, and I had no reason not to be. I thanked Mummy tons of times and hung up to call Ayra back. She was still at her friend's house and was not expecting a call from me.

'My family and I have no issues with whatever your past has in it, Ayra. I just spoke to my mother,' I assured her.

'Let us talk in Bengaluru. I will be there later this week,' she proposed, and I agreed.

CHAPTER 11

Three days later . . .

I saw her standing at a coffee shop near my house. Bhanu and I had met each other accidentally outside my building and were chatting about Delhi and other general things when I spotted her.

'That's her,' I told Bhanu, and it took him less than a few seconds to understand to whom I was referring. 'Which one? The one is black trousers?' He was even able to spot her without assistance.

'Yes, that is Ayra,' I grinned from ear to ear.

'She is so pretty! Now I know why you have been so crazy about her all this time! So, what are you guys planning for the evening? You told me that you would meet her for coffee late at night, but it is just six in the evening!' Bhanu teased me.

Ayra was in the city for a meeting, and we had planned to meet after her dinner with her colleagues at work got over. To my surprise, she texted me and asked me for my exact address half an hour ago, and there she was. 'Let me go and ask her,' I said to Bhanu and before he could stop me, I was leaping to greet her, ignoring that he had to be introduced to her as well.

'Hi, what a pleasant surprise!' I told her, soaking in her radiance. She looked paler and thinner than the last time I had seen her, which in measured time was not very long ago. 'You have lost weight again!' I couldn't help but remark, and she raised her eyebrows at me.

'Lost weight as in good that I have lost weight or bad that I have lost weight?' she quizzed me, trying to put me in a spot. I just shrugged my shoulders as I didn't like that she had lost weight—she looked underfed. So, without commenting on it further, I asked her why she was there at that hour as she had a meeting all day and we were to meet in the evening. 'The meeting got over earlier than expected, and I had some extra time at hand. I go back home tomorrow morning by the way,' she told me. I immediately took the cue to ask her out for a coffee date.

By this time, Bhanu had joined us. 'Yes, we can all go together,' he piped in. 'I am Bhanu, by the way, his friend. I live nearby with my boyfriend Pathak,' he said and observed Ayra's reactions. Bhanu does this all the time; whenever he meets a new acquaintance who has the possibility of becoming a friend, he straight up tells them that he is gay. 'It saves a lot of time and effort, you know!' he told me when I'd once asked him why. 'People sometimes have prejudices, which impact their choice of friends,' he elaborated. When Ayra smiled warmly and extended her hand to shake with Bhanu's, I knew that they would be friends for life—and they were. 'And he lives in this building,' Bhanu pointed at my house on the top floor.

'Really?' Ayra looked at the high-rise for a while before I interjected her thoughts and asked her to accompany me and only me for a cup of coffee. Bhanu bid us goodbye after it was decided that we were all meeting again for dinner that night at Bhanu and Pathak's home, which was a rented accommodation.

'But why at your place and not at mine?' I asked him over a text.

'Because she wouldn't have come to your house, you duffer!' came his reply and I agreed with him. If I had proposed dinner at my place, she would have asked to be fed at a restaurant instead, which meant there would be no privacy.

That evening, Ayra and I chatted for a few hours over coffee and chai. She spoke about her interesting work-life, while I bored her with my college nonsense. 'Where have you reached with the book?' she asked me casually.

'Halfway,' I replied, looking at my coffee, and lying like a pro. I told her that my father wanted me to join his business soon and she couldn't agree more with him.

'Have you told him about your plans for this MBA?' she asked me, looking straight into my eyes, and I couldn't lie.

'I did once but will have to do that again as the conversation in the past had lead to nothing,' I told her honestly and she nodded understandingly, stirring her coffee with the tiny spoon. She took two packets of sugar for her coffee while I took none for my chai.

'You know, quitting is not as bad as we make it out to be. Sometimes, we take decisions based on impulses and then we do not want to pursue those because of rationality and what the world says about quitting. We have only one life, so I think it is okay to decide to quit. Do not think of what people will say as they don't have to live your life. You do,' she said to me again, assuring me that she stood by my decisions, and I couldn't have agreed more with her. I felt more confidence in me.

'We have only one life and we sometimes make bad decisions. It is okay to back off; it is alright to quit if we want to,' I repeated in my head a few times as I had to blurt out the same lines in front of Papa when I told him.

I dropped Ayra at her hotel at seven to pick her up again at eight-thirty. We were headed to Bhanu's and Prateek's home. When I went there on a bike, which I had loaned from a friend to pick her up again, I saw her come down the stairs as I waited for her at the reception. She was staying at the second floor. She looked like a dream, dressed in an orange salwar-suit, with her hair loose and a little makeup adding to the glow on her face. Looking at her walk down the lobby of the hotel, my resolve to go back to Delhi became stronger. 'I have to live my life with her,' I told my heart again and the sooner I spoke to my parents the better it would be.

Ayra was initially reluctant to sit on the bike in a suit. But a few adjustments of poses later, it was a smooth ride that ended sooner than I had wanted it to. She held me tightly at my waist with one hand holding down her dress. I looked at her through the rear-view mirror as I drove.

She smiled at my compliments, blushed when I told her that I loved her and laughed at my jokes unaware that I was capturing her beauty in my heart forever, through her reflections in the bike's mirror.

We came to a halt at the small but very earthy and beautiful house that Bhanu and Pathak had been calling home for the past two years. The house belonged to an NRI couple, who lived in London. After many people refused to rent their home to a gay couple, they had to resort to a lie to secure this place. Unsure of just how fussy the NRI couple was about who lived there, they applied for tenancy as cousins and offered a higher than usual rent amount claiming that they needed a place urgently.

We walked past the rusty main door, which led to a small kitchen garden. Bhanu, the artist, is also Bhanu, the gardener. He is very fond of anything that grows from the soil and loves growing his own veggies. Their main door was ajar, and as we walked closer, we could figure out that the usually much-in-love couple was fighting over garam masala!

That evening, to everyone's surprise, Bhanu had cooked a vegetarian treat for his special guest Ayra. He had really liked her after their first meeting and wanted to make an impression on her. He had been messaging me, again and again, all evening, pressurizing me to ask her if she wanted to be with me, for life. I had not told anyone that I had said it thrice already to her. It was very personal, and no matter how good a friend Bhanu was, there were a few things that I wanted to keep only between Ayra and me.

We were welcomed inside very warmly, and Ayra met
Pathak for the first time. We had set our foot in their house
at eight-forty in the night, and fifteen minutes later, Ayra
was already helping out the hosts in the kitchen while I was
browsing through their magazines in the cozy living area.
I had been there on many occasions, but each time I was
there, the house was full of people—people unknown to me.
It was the first time that I was at their home with someone
I knew. I looked around to see if there was anything that
I could explore while the three of them cooked in the
kitchen. I finally found a few sports magazines stuffed in a
corner and started flipping through their pages. I was able
to hear their laughter fill the house and could do nothing
better than be jealous and feel useless, sitting in a corner
looking at sports cars that I had no reason to be looking at.
I do not enjoy the process of cooking as such, while Ayra
found it to be very relaxing. 'It soothes my soul,' she said,
when I asked her why.

After I got bored with the magazines and started
exploring more things around me, I soon figured out
their music system, and a few minutes later, the cooking
party, including Ayra was grooving to my favourite cheesy
Bollywood numbers. At around nine-thirty, the three cooks
finally came out with a piping hot dinner, which was served
with much love and camaraderie. All of us had a hearty meal
with a lovely conversation around Indians living abroad.

A lot of jokes were cracked, and we spent one of the
most beautiful evenings of our courtship period in great
company, along with some amazing vegetarian food. After
the meal, the two love birds gave us a mini-break from

them. They had forgotten to arrange a customary sweet dish and had to hop out of the house to get some ice cream. 'Vanilla for me and chocolate for her,' I told Bhanu and looked at Ayra, as she gave me a warm smile of approval. 'At least I knew this right!' I remembered her favourite ice cream because of my birthday parties, which she attended.

'I am sorry about my crazy friends,' I apologized after they left. I knew that she liked them as well.

'Don't be silly!' she responded, and looked down at her hands. She said something very softly. I couldn't comprehend even a word of it, so I moved a little closer to her, very carefully, ensuring not to scare her. Realizing that I had hearing troubles, she repeated what she had said a little louder this time, 'I wish I had friends like them, too . . . ' Her words melted my heart, and I couldn't resist holding her tight.

'You have me. Oh! I love you so much,' the last bit escaped my mouth unintentionally, in the spur of the moment. Immediately I feared that she might withdraw herself again, but she did not. I felt her grip tighten around my shoulders as she held me.

We stood like that for a while as I repeated the words a few times. She still did not reply to me but her touch gave me the response that I needed. We realized that our hosts might not come back anytime soon so hand in hand we walked out of the backdoor into their lovely backyard. They had a beautiful hammock, a few chairs, a couple of wooden tables, and some flower pots, making the space appear warm and friendly. I offered her a seat at the table but she chose to lie in the hammock instead and gaze at the stars. I moved a wooden chair next to the hammock and parked myself on it to be close to her. I was close enough so that I could see her face light up as she witnessed the stars twinkle in the sky and talked about them as if they were the most precious things in the universe. Maybe they were . . .

'What are stars, according to you?' she asked me a bizarre question a little while later.

'Balls of fire!' I gave an out-of-the-book response that made her cringe.

'Your answer is what you have been told what the stars are. Have you seen them be balls of fire? To you, do they appear like balls of fire? They are anything but a yellow or orange-like sun, which is a ball of fire,' she told me, moving her finger up and down as if giving me a lecture in school.

I shrugged my shoulders and tossed the question back to her to hear her thoughts on it. 'Okay, fine. I am wrong then. What are stars, according to you?'

'I believe that people who are too good for the earth, leave the planet and become stars,' she said.

Her answer gave birth to my next question, 'What about people who are not that good? Where do they go?'

I saw her smile, not just with her lips but with her eyes. 'They are born again and again and again until they learn how to be good.'

'Ah! That made sense. She would be a great writer one day,' I told myself. I just knew it.

Both of us giggled, and the moment froze in my memory as a high-definition picture hung in my eyes. Every time I close them, I see the same moment, again and again, just like it is.

'Do you want to talk to me or someone else about . . . you know . . . ' I spoke after a pause and immediately regretted it.

Her face changed colours; she got up and ran into the washroom. When she came out, she looked flushed again, like she did at McDonald's. 'Are you okay?' I asked her with concern, and she nodded, with a weak smile. I knew that she was not okay. *Why doesn't she talk about it? Why doesn't she talk about anything?*

She slumped into the hammock and signalled me to join her. I did as I was asked as I believed that she was comfortable with me around her. She did appear to be so, then why was she not talking?

As soon as I joined her, she held my hand and said, 'I do not like talking about my sorrows, my past or my memories. I get addicted to them; I get sucked into all the negativity, and there is so much to life than all that has happened already. Let us get addicted to the future and the joy it holds instead. Tell me, what brings you joy?'

Until our hosts came back, we spoke at length about what gives her happiness and what books we were currently reading. We discussed my love for travel and her wish to travel. I made a mental note to take her to Sydney one day, as she wanted to go there once in her life. She told me about her aspiration to work for children and contribute towards a healthy future for the coming generations. I spoke about my perfect family and my status of being a pampered child. She kind of knew it all along—I am definitely not as difficult to interpret as I would want myself to be.

Ayra was, in her own words, 'always overshadowed' by her overachieving sister and was never loved enough by her new parents. They didn't want to take up the responsibility as they had a daughter of their own and wanted a son, too. After a few miscarriages, her new parents decided to stop trying, and they were stuck with Ayra for life, as after being freed from prison, her father decided to remarry. I felt sad for her, but that was a part of her life that I could do nothing about. While I lived surrounded by loved ones, she always struggled to prove herself to be worthy of love. Before our conversation became too heavy again, Bhanu and Pathak came back home, and all four of us had ice cream, which had taken forever to arrive. I was glad that they gave us the much-needed time alone, though. Finally, I dropped Ayra back to her hotel on my bike. She sat on the backseat and slowly hummed some old Hindi songs.

'Will you ever tell me or will I have to wait until eternity?' I asked her at the steps of her hotel. It was two in the night and there was no one apart from the receptionist near us.

'Tell you what?' she was sleepy and yet was still teasing me.

'You know what,' I replied, and hung my head in disappointment.

She leaned onto me and kissed me goodnight, on my cheek. 'I love you, brat, so it is, yes!' she said and from then on we were kind of together. She never said it aloud though—it was just a murmur, low enough to be nothing.

CHAPTER 12

After I had confessed my feelings to Ayra, Mummy wanted a minute by minute account of what was happening between Ayra and me, and why I was taking forever to take the next step—involving the families. I had already checked a few times with Ayra, and it was very well-established that neither of us felt a need to reconsider our feelings. Therefore, I decided to talk to my father before I spoke to her family. I kind of knew that he was already aware of the affair and was waiting for me to come and talk to him. My parents do not keep any secrets from each other, mainly because Mummy is a big fan of gossip and is also one of the worst at keeping secrets. So, when I called Papa to talk to him about Ayra, he knew it all. He had met her too and approved of her. My mother's habit of letting out secrets did me a favour, as I was no longer under the pressure of figuring out a way to talk about her family to my parents. There were more than a few skeletons in Ayra's closet and thankfully, Papa was okay with them too. All he wanted was to see us happy together.

The next step was to involve her family, and even though I had almost no regard for her parents after knowing how they treated her, I knew how much their approval meant to her. So, I called Ayra and told her that I was now planning to move forward and wanted to know her thoughts on it. She was happy, but it was not an 'over the moon' kind of happy. She was scared of what her parents would say and how they would react to the affair. 'I will tell them that I love you,' I told her, and waited for her to say something. When she gave me nothing more than a verbal nod, I added, 'And that you love me, too.'

'You won't. They will kill me,' she told me angrily.

'But you do love me, right?' I had to really dig it out of her as I was losing my patience.

'Kind of,' she replied and then giggled hard.

'What do you mean by "kind of" love?' I asked her, irritated.

'"Kind of" means "kind of". Now go to sleep, you brat,' she said and hung up on me.

So, the next day I took another flight to Delhi and spoke to my mother first in the absence of my father. She was over the moon when she heard that I had finally found enough courage to go and talk to her parents. My parents had told me that they were more than happy to talk to Ayra's family and send out a formal marriage proposal, but I wanted to talk to them first. While I thought that I was most eager to get out of the MBA and get married to Ayra, my father was the one who wanted to initiate a talk with her parents as soon as possible and get us married within the next few weeks. Apparently, the days were auspicious, and the match was 'made in heaven' as per the family pandit. They agreed to wait until I had spoken to her family. Mummy declared that I had to get married soon and also move back to Delhi as soon as possible. Papa echoed her thoughts as well, and finally, MBA was off my back. I wasted no time and packed my bags, bid my goodbyes, and took the next flight home.

After coming back to Delhi permanently, a week later on a Sunday, I messaged Ayra to ask her parents if I could come over. Usually, in India, the families meet each other and decide the fate of a couple, but I was going to break tradition. 'Imagine what you would tell our kids about how we got married?' she giggled over the phone and I laughed along.

'I will tell them that your parents were nasty,' I said and she got angry.

'Why do you have to say such things about them?'

'Don't you know why? How can you not see how badly they have treated you?' I protested.

'See,' she started explaining calmly, 'when one goes to a mine, it is very easy to find coal all around you. Be someone who can find a diamond in a coal mine; look for the good and you will be able to see it. My parents gave me a place to live, they paid my fees, gave me equal opportunity like they did to their own daughter. They let me live the kind of life my mother would have wanted me to live even when my father was a killer.' Her tone was flat and I couldn't gauge her state of mind. So, I apologized and told her that I shall be there to meet her parents at five in the evening.

The real reason why I wanted to meet her parents before they met my family was that I wanted them to hear directly from me how much I cared for and loved their daughter and how I was going to prove to be the best man for her. I expected them to ask a lot of questions, and I was prepared to answer them to their satisfaction. I wanted to do all of this before my parents got a chance to meet them. From what I had gathered from Ayra, they were not very excited to meet me or my family. They wanted a boy from their own caste for Ayra, just like for her elder sister Somya. When Ayra told them about my parents and their religious backgrounds, friction was to be expected. I didn't want the families to meet before I got a chance to diffuse the fire.

As agreed upon, sharp at five, I reached their doorstep. Ayra opened the door for me, and she looked every bit scared as I was. 'Hi,' she said, and escorted me into their living room. I was greeted coldly by her mother, who came out of the kitchen, wiping her hands on a kitchen towel. She told me that Ayra's father was still at work and would not be able to meet me. I was very well aware that Ayra's mother made all the decisions in their home, so I was not disappointed much. Leaving me in her mother's company, Ayra went into the kitchen to get me a glass of water. I had not even taken a seat by then. Her mother took a seat on the brown leather sofa and asked me to sit down as well. Carefully, I placed the fruit basket that I brought over for the family at the centre of the table and sat on the sofa opposite to her mother. And thus, the round of interrogation began.

How old was I?
How educated was I?
Did I have any plans to go and live abroad?

Did my parents know about us?

What religious backgrounds did my parents have?

Will I force Ayra to change her name or convert to a different religion after marriage?

What were my plans for my future?

Even though I knew that her mother was aware of most of the things that she asked me about, I remained as calm and composed as possible and responded well to all her queries. She was not fond of me. She found interactions with me overwhelming, and that reflected in her tone as she spoke to me. I had gone there to avoid any prejudices that her family could have had against mine, but I ended up making it worse.

I took a leave from her half an hour later, when she ran out of questions, and no dinner or tea invite was extended my way. Ayra came to the main door downstairs to bid me goodbye, and it felt as if it was our last goodbye. I knew that she would never go against her parents' wishes, and her mother definitely didn't wish her to be with me.

'She didn't like me much, did she?' I asked her honestly, and she nodded.

'Why?' I asked out of curiosity, as I had been quite polite to her even when she had asked me some rude questions in nasty tones.

'I think they are worried as you guys are wealthy and we can't afford a lavish wedding,' she told me, and I ran back upstairs to say one last thing to her mother, leaving Ayra at the main gate.

When I came back a few minutes later, she looked puzzled and asked me what I had said.

'I will tell you later if she agrees to our marriage,' I didn't want to raise her hopes very high, even though it was the most positive I had been all evening.

By the time I reached home, there was a message on my phone from Ayra to say that her mother wanted to meet my parents. 'Yes!' I shouted and hit my fist in the air. My parents were more than thrilled to meet Ayra's parents the next week.

'What did you tell her?' Ayra kept messaging me again and again. I couldn't tell her that I had told her mother that my family would bear all the expenses for the wedding, and that was when she agreed to the match readily. Her parents were worried about their own future. They didn't want to spend a lot of money on her wedding, especially because Ayra was not their own daughter. After I assured her mother that they did not have to spend any money, she connected with Ayra's father, and soon it was decided that I was indeed a perfect match for Ayra. I had also promised her mother that it was not to be a grand affair. It was difficult for me to convince my parents that their only son was to get married without any fireworks. They agreed at one condition—they would throw a larger-than-life reception party. That was something to which I could not object.

The two families met, and much to my surprise, the meeting went on smoothly. I met her father for the first time when they came to our house. They had not brought Ayra with them as it was supposedly bad luck for the girl to be visiting her soon-to-be home before marriage. I was amazed at how little her father spoke, and how much her mother did. He looked happy to be at our house and was the one who initiated talks around a 'ring ceremony'. My parents couldn't have been happier, while Ayra's mother looked indifferent. My parents loved Ayra so much that they didn't mind her parents. It was decided that a small ring ceremony was to be planned for the coming week and a wedding ceremony, fifteen days later.

I urged my parents to opt for a simple wedding, so that Ayra's parents were not burdened financially at all. While my father wanted a grand wedding for his only son, he did understand my concern and agreed. That day, the families decided to perform a north Indian custom of 'Roka', where the girl's and the boy's families declare their wishes of getting their kids married to each other. The next day, the families met again at a temple near Ayra's house, and a small amount of cash was exchanged as a symbol of luck while both the boy and the girl were given blessings.

After the quick and hurried 'Roka' ceremony, everyone had departed to their own homes. After reaching home, my worried Papa took me aside and asked me if I was aware that Ayra's mother didn't like me much. Much to his surprise, I confessed that I was mindful of her indifference towards me. Relieved, he retired into his room, and I disappeared into mine. I texted my wife-to-be to check if she was happy and if all was peaceful at their home. It was.

As there was very little time between the first meeting of our families and the wedding, Ayra and I could not meet each other after the Roka, until the day of engagement.

I saw her dressed in a light-pink saree and it instantly became my favourite colour. The function was arranged at one of Papa's friend's farmhouse, so that the bride's family had to bear no expenses. The party, which included Ayra, her parents, one of her cousins, the cousin's husband and his family, came to the place half an hour late than expected and by then the priest had declared that the 'shubh muhurat'(auspicious time) was nearly over. Even though we had been talking and texting a lot for the past week, I felt that we had not been in touch as much as I would have liked to be. I wanted to talk to my shy bride at least once, but with the priest losing his cool and both the families disagreeing over the traditions and customs, all we could manage were a few worried glances in each other's direction.

Usually, the wedding day and the days before it are full of fun, frolic, laughter, and happiness, but I could not wait for these days to get over and finally be married to her. Every passing day was like walking on a landmine, which was waiting to burst. On every occasion, her mother expressed her unhappiness; her relatives tried to prove again and again how different we were from them and how confusing our religious makeup was; and worst of it all, her father hardly said anything to control the situation. With many bloopers and a few rounds of scolding from the priest, the ring ceremony was finally done. 'Only one more ceremony to go!' I reminded myself, 'Just a few more days and this was all going to be over.' I was one of the few people who looked forward to a marriage more than the wedding.

5 November 2017
D–Day

Our wedding day was lovely. Unlike most people who opt for evening or night weddings in India, Ayra and I decided to get married while the sun was still up. Our wedding was to take place at twelve in the noon. All the excitement and happiness kept me wide awake the night before. My house was full of guests from all over the country. Papa and Mummy had decided to make the mehendi ceremony a grand event as the actual wedding was an intimate affair.

Ayra, too, had her mehendi ceremony at her home, which meant that she and I could barely talk that day. I sent her a few lovely messages, and she replied in a few words, as her mehendi ceremony had begun earlier than mine. By the end of the event, I was exhausted, so I retired to my bedroom while the rest of the party still danced to Punjabi numbers. Despite being so darn tired, I could not rest. I wondered what she must be doing and how her mehendi was going to look the next day. I looked at mine—a circle with 'S & A' written on it—and grinned foolishly. This was it. We were getting married in a few hours and then we were to be with each other, forever.

After a few hours of waiting, I gave up on any hope to get a call or message for her. She was busy, and I knew it, but still, sleep was not at all on my mind. The clock kept on going 'tick-tock' and I felt myself going into a state where I was asleep and yet fully aware of my surroundings. I was dreaming of our honeymoon in Sydney—a dream of hers that I wanted to fulfil. Not very long afterwards, I woke up because of the alarm clock and my cousins barging into my room. It was seven in the morning, and some more wedding rituals had to be done before I could take a shower.

I checked my phone—still nothing.

Sharp at eleven, dressed in a sherwani, I walked out of the house with the other family members, to bring her home.

It was to be a quiet wedding ceremony at the same temple near her house where we had our Roka ceremony done. As soon as I got down from the car, I saw my bride. Dressed in a mustard-coloured suit with a heavy red dupatta covering her head, she stood in the temple with some of her relatives. Not looking anything like a conventional bride, she took my breath away. I realized that I was overdressed as compared to her, but I didn't care. My father kept his hand on my shoulder to boost my confidence and signalled that we walk into the temple. The families greeted each other and Ayra, and I sat next to each other at the havan kund. Everything else was just like any other Hindu wedding ceremony, with one difference—it was all done at a super-fast speed. We were done with it all in half an hour and knelt down to touch the feet of both our parents.

Fifteen minutes later, after a not-so-emotional goodbye, I was sitting in my car with my wife. I saw her weeping silently and held her hand. 'I love you; you know that, right?' I told her with a smile, and she lifted her eyes to meet mine. She nodded, and I pressed her hand. It was all done—we were married. She was Mrs Ayra Malhotra now.

The Present
August 2018

Today, as I sit behind my desk, trying to write and rewrite some more of my story, I feel a constant but indefinable pain in my chest. It is a sort of pain that makes one feel alive; it makes one feel aware of the heart that is beating within one's chest; makes one feel thankful for life and also tells them that the human body reacts to not just the food that feeds it, but also the thoughts that feed the brain. I have been trepidatious lately. Ayra doesn't know, or at least I hope that she doesn't. I have started feeling the brunt of all the thoughts that have been running through my head, screeching and making it unbearable for me to be sane for long. I have been worried about the future for long, but I always thought that the future was not something that would hit us for many years to come. Suddenly, it has occurred to me that maybe the future that I have been dreading is not very far away. It might be closer than I can imagine it to be. It feels closer than I want it to be, and it is moving towards us at a very high speed. I am not in control of things, and this irks me the most. No matter how much I want to help her, all I can do is stand in a corner and watch her fade away in front of my eyes. She has been stronger than me, way stronger than I can ever be.

The new drug has stopped working.

It was not as miraculous as the doctor had hoped it to be. He thinks this is it, but this can't be it. I have been researching day and night, but it looks like we have reached the end of the tunnel, and now there is no hope, no flicker, and no light. When I said goodnight to her tonight, she corrected me, 'Start saying goodbye from now on, brat. I might not be sticking around for long, as I am too tired to continue with this . . .' Her words had a hint of humour in them, but I fail to see anything funny about a goodbye. They are not what I want in my life. How can I say goodbye just yet? She is so young; we had planned to live together, travel the world and then grow old in each other's company. How can I say goodbye just yet? I am not ready, not now.

Struggling to keep my head in place, I got up to sip some water. I need distraction no matter how small or big, as long as it kept me away from my never-ending train of thoughts. I walk into the kitchen and find a note stuck to the refrigerator. 'When does she get time to write them and then put them at places for me to find,' I wondered and opened the unsealed envelope. In her handwriting, was another note, which she wanted to read to me the next day, I am sure.

She knew all that was going in my head, she always did.

To You,

Remember I once told you that I would love you forever and you asked me what does 'forever' even mean?

I didn't know how to put it in words then, but I do know now. I will be taking a dose of my new medicine and would be sleeping like a horse by the time you come back from work, and I cannot risk holding on to it until morning. So here it goes:

When two hearts fall in love, there is nothing else but a constant need to be close to one another. The need to hold

*hands; to hear their heart beating under your palm, and trace
their smile with your fingertips. Such cravings, and such needs,
carve paths for two hearts in love to travel on, so that they
can travel forever. Forever has no clocks, no notion of time or
distance. Forever happens when it just feels natural to be with
one another all the time.*

*You are mine forever. Also, it is never a mere accident that
two hearts like ours find each other. It is much more than that;
it is destiny. You are my destiny, and it is in your destiny to be
with me till my last breath.*

With Love.

15 November 2017
Sydney

'I hope you are not nervous,' I asked her jokingly for the
n-th time, and she gave me the same look that she had been
giving me in response to my question since I had started
asking it. It had been ten days that we had been married,
but this was the first time that we were truly alone, just the
two of us with no one to come in between us. I could not
control my laughter and gave out a snort. Ayra widened her
big eyes, indicating that she had enough of the same joke.

Ayra had told me that she wanted to go to Sydney and
I decided to make her wish come true as a wedding present.
So, on the night of our wedding, I presented her two tickets
to Sydney. I was expecting her to be overwhelmed and to
hug me with excitement. She was overwhelmed, but not

because she was happy or excited, but because she got scared. I saw her nervously looking at the tickets and asked her if she was okay with my plans. 'You want to go to Sydney, right?' I felt the need to ask her, judging by her expression.

'Yes . . . yes, of course,' she replied unsurely.

'What is it?' I couldn't help asking her. Honestly, at that moment, I was ready to cancel the trip if she was going to be that upset over it.

'How long is the flight?' she asked me after a few seconds.

'Sixteen hours.'

'Okay, I need to tell you something,' came her reply. 'I have never been on such a long flight,' she confessed.

'Which is alright, there is a first time for everything.' I looked at her innocent face and cupped it with both my hands. 'Do you want to go?' I asked her again seriously, even though I knew that she was getting worried unnecessarily.

'Can we go by ship?' she was really scared, but I couldn't help but laugh.

'Are you kidding me? By ship?' I hugged her tight and she struggled in my embrace trying to get free. 'What is so funny?' she asked, feeling annoyed, and I immediately stopped my laughter.

'Nothing is funny. I know it can sound scary but once in the air, you won't feel a thing, I promise.' I tried my best to bring her mind at peace but she had her inhibitions. That night was spent making her aware of how it was all safe and why air travel was safer than sea travel. She was worried that the pilot might doze off while flying the plane as it was a really long duration to be awake at a stretch.

'It is just sixteen hours,' I told her again and again.

After that night, we had a reception, and then for four nights we were hosted continuously by someone or the other for dinner. This exhausted us so much that we returned home at one or two at night with energy just enough to take us to the bedroom, without crashing on the way. On the fifth day, Ayra went back to live with her family for the next three days, as per custom. On the night before we were to head over to Sydney, she returned from home, nervous as heck about the flight the next day. I tried to make her feel better for a while, but soon my queries related to her wellness and preparedness for the flight started irritating her.

When we reached the Delhi airport, we had a seven-member party accompanying us: Papa, Mummy, Bhanu and Pathak, as they could not attend the wedding, two of my cousins and our house help, who had become very fond of the new mistress of the house. As soon as we entered the airport, she clung on to me for life. As amusing as it was, I also found the situation very romantic. Ayra held on to my right sleeve—not the arm, just the sleeve, like always— as we moved around, checking in, dropping our bags, going through security, etc. She refused to eat or drink. Thankfully, soon after takeoff, her anxiety subsided. She still held on to my hand as we looked outside the window. 'It is surreal, this machine will fly for twelve hours straight with no break and the same pilot,' she murmured as we flew above the sky, and looking at her, I agreed. It was, indeed, surreal. A few months ago, who could have believed that in such a short period, we would not just be in love like we

were, but also get married. My life had completely turned
around. From a boy who ran away from responsibilities, I
had become a man willing to help his father unburden his
responsibilities. I was regularly going to the office now and
had taken only two days off for my own wedding. Ayra
was on a month-long leave from her office; she wanted
to continue working, and I was in favour of it; however,
I did believe that her work could be more useful for our
company. I wanted her to take up a role in Papa's business;
it was, in fact, suggested by Papa himself, who was not sure
how to bring the topic up. He wanted her to take up the
finance department, so he set me up for the task. I planned
to ask her about her thoughts on the same towards the end
of the trip.

The long plane journey went by in a moment as we
chatted our way through. Somewhere over the Indian
Ocean, Ayra saw the humour in the entire situation and
much before we landed, I began teasing her about her
unnecessary fear of long flights.

We touched down at Sydney and headed straight to our
hotel at Darling Harbour. It was seven in the morning, and
the sun was partly hidden by the clouds. The weather was
a little warmer than we expected, but it was perfect to head
over to a beach. So, I rang the reception and asked the guy
on the phone 'Aron' to suggest a beach nearby. 'Sir, I can
arrange a cab to take you guys to Bondi Beach,' he said.

Ayra was in the washroom, changing her clothes when
I knocked on the door gently. 'One minute,' she said softly
and walked out of the door dressed in a floral maxi dress.
In the last couple of days, with so much happening in and

around us, I had completely forgotten to take notice of how beautiful she was and how much she was glowing since the wedding.

'Are you hungry? Shall we grab breakfast before we head to the beach?' I asked her, saying each word carefully and slowly, so that I didn't fumble as I was too mesmerized by her at that moment.

'I am too tired,' she said and lied down on the very comfy-looking and inviting bed of our honeymoon suite. The crimson bedsheets were very tempting. 'But we have to see Sydney, she wants to see the place,' I told myself.

Just when I was about to come out of my state of numbness caused by her beauty, Ayra patted her hand on the bedsheets, inviting me further into the trance that I was already in. That was the end of it. Sometime later, we heard and ignored the phone call and then the knock on our door. Bondi Beach had to wait, for some time at least.

Despite being married, I was shy about certain things. So, when I called the reception again, I hoped that Aron was off duty, which he wasn't. I apologized for earlier and asked him if a cab could be arranged later that evening to take us to Bondi Beach. We were neither the first honeymooners at the hotel nor the first ones ever to cancel a cab request. He happily obliged, and I made a note to give him a generous tip on our departure. We had woken up in the afternoon and were jet-lagged, so I ordered food into the room for us and then jumped straight back into bed to join my new wife. It was a novel feeling, and I wanted the feeling never to leave us.

Bondi Beach
New South Wales, Australia

One of the most memorable evenings of our honeymoon
was spent on this beach. When we reached there for the
very first time, it was too crowded for my comfort; tourists
and locals filled the beach for as far as our eyes could see.
But slowly, as time passed by, and it was time for the sun
to go down and melt into the sea, we witnessed the crowd
of tourists and families dispersing. Lone surfers, lovers of
sunsets and people like us, who were there just to absorb
the beauty of the place, remained scattered on the sandy
beaches to witness the sun submerging into the ocean,
leaving behind no traces of its existence, as it became one
with the ocean. Ayra loved talking about everything in the
sky, so she described the sunset like a poet for me, and I
sat at the beach listening to her talk about their love affair.
She believed that the sun was a shy lover, who submerged
into the waters to ensure that no one gets to know of its
affair with the earth. When we think that the sun is gone,
it is actually hiding until the world sleeps and then when
everyone is gone, the sun flirts with the earth through a
mirror, which we know as the moon. Her theories were
pure madness, and yet, they made all the sense in the world.
Now, I cannot see the sun, the earth and the moon as the
objects we were led to believe them to be. I see them as
lovers; I see them in love.

Minute by minute, the sky above us changed colour,
from blue to hues of pink and yellow and then finally red.
As the changes took place slowly, we could only marvel

at all the things around us, which were inexplicable. We were awestruck in each other's arms as we witnessed the vibrant, carefully blended colour combination presented in front of our eyes. Traces of pink, blue, grey, white, yellow and many more were being painted into life by nature—all shades of love and all shades of life.

I loved addressing Ayra as my wife. *Can I please get two glasses of iced tea for my wife and me? My wife and I love Australia. My wife always wanted to visit Sydney, so here we are, on our honeymoon.* I chatted with a few other people at a bar near the beach after the sunset while I continued looking at her from the corner of my eyes, as she lovingly waited for my return. One great thing about the place was that people around, the workers as well as the natives, were really helpful. Whenever we lost our way or needed to find a place, there were more than enough people to help us out. Sydney, like most metropolitan cities, never sleeps and as our hotel was right in the middle of the city, it made it easier for us to stay out late and step out at any time during the nights.

That evening, after a few mocktails, we headed back to the beach from the beach bar. The air was refreshing, and it smelled of the ocean. It was dark, yet, many seagulls flew really low, trying to catch their supper. We parked ourselves at the foot of the beach, so that the sea could touch us.

'Hungry?' I asked Ayra, whose head was resting on my shoulders, as we enjoyed the beauty and the sound of the sea.

'Very,' she replied dramatically, while rubbing her belly. We looked around to see what our options were.

I didn't want to head back to the same bar, as they had only grilled seafood options, and my wife was a vegetarian. Unlike beaches in India, where one can see a lot of food vendors around, this place had no restaurants nearby. Upon enquiry, we were suggested to go to a place called the 'Bondi Icebergs Club'. It is a place where you can literally eat by the sea. 'Sounds fun,' said my partner, and that was enough for us to head over and try it out. On our way there, I quickly checked on my phone if they had a vegetarian selection, and thankfully they did.

I will not bore you much with a lot of details about the place or the surrounding; all that I will tell you is that we had a fantastic dinner and a lovely time at the Icebergs.

During our fifteen-day trip, we spent not less than five romantic evenings at Bondi Beach, absorbing the beauty of the wonders of nature around us. At that time of the year, the air was clean and refreshing, so Ayra and I took frequent walks around the city at different times of the day. Her health was excellent the whole time, and I had not witnessed any stress in her behaviour.

We visited the beautiful Blue Mountains, the Palm Beach, the iconic Sydney Opera House, the Coogee Beach, the Manly Beach and many others places. Every evening, we would come back and park ourselves at an Indian restaurant called 'Manjit's', to savour their Indian cuisine and talk about ourselves and our life once we moved back home.

However, on the last day of our honeymoon, when we were coming back in the ferry from the Opera House after dinner, I witnessed for the very first time what Ayra called an 'anxiety attack'. The last time I had nearly seen her sick was at McDonald's, and on that day, she had run into the washroom. This time, as we were on the ferry crossing the sea, she had no place to run but to be there.

While I chatted happily and pointed towards the skyline, she went quiet for a while. I asked her if she was okay, but she lied to me even when I could see that she was not. 'What is wrong?' I asked her worriedly, as she went pale within seconds, right in front of my eyes. I reached out to hold her hand, and her sticky cold fingers trembled in mine. The air that evening was cold, but not as cold as it had been for the many days that we were in the city. Her fingers tightened into a fist, and I felt her hands sweating. 'Are you okay?' I repeated my question a few times. The ferry was nearly at the dock, and I knew that a cab or an Uber could be hailed from just around the corner to go to a doctor.

Ayra had not said a word or even blinked her eyes. Her eyes were wide open, and her lips shut tight. Just as the ferry was docking, she let go of my hand and rushed towards the railing of the ferry to throw up. I held her hand and swiped her hair away from her face. Some moments later, after she was done, I offered her water, which she sipped. Her face was full of sweat beads, and she was shivering. 'Let us go to a doctor,' I declared, and she said nothing. I took it as a 'yes' and called an Uber as soon as we got off the ferry.

I checked online and could find a medical centre some half an hour away from where we were. I entered the address of the medical centre into the app as our destination when our Uber arrived. Ayra looked very sick, and I was clueless as I had never really taken care of an ill person

Slowly, the cab moved towards the busy roads, and we merged into swelling traffic. We were more than fifteen minutes away from the medical centre when it started again. The cab driver looked back at us through the rear-view mirror and suggested that we make a stop. He didn't want her to throw up in his cab and I didn't want her to throw up at all.

She signalled me to pull down the glass of the window, and I did so. She breathed in a lot of air. I adjusted myself and moved to the other side. She now sat at the window, and the driver stopped the car at a parking space. 'Do you want to get down and get some medicine from the pharmacy?' the driver suggested, as I was patting her back.

'Please do not do this,' she looked at me and said, hinting that I should keep my hands off her. I nodded a few times and removed my hand from her back as it was making her condition worse. Just then, she rushed out of the cab. I didn't want to embarrass her, so I didn't follow her. I knew what she was doing. I was worried for her to say the least, but she deserved her privacy, and I gave her just that.

She came back looking for some water. The driver helped her with a bottle of water, and she vanished again at the back of the car. 'Is there a pharmacy nearby?' I asked him.

'Yes, there are a few in the city, but I am not sure if any doctors would be available at this hour, mate! There is a hospital just there, too. Do you have insurance?' he asked in a very thick accent.

I had urged Ayra more than a few times already to see another doctor as her doctor was no good. But then

I had never really taken her to someone better. I was not very persistent about my requests as I somewhere believed that she would be magically cured as soon as she and I got married. Well, the magic didn't happen, and she did need to see a good doctor. I had visited her doctor with her the last time, and all that she did was prescribe a few antidepressants. I wanted to tell her that she doesn't look depressed, and that she shouldn't be depressed either, but then memories of her past and her notes in her drawing books came to me, and I realized that probably she was depressed; probably she was hiding it all very well most of the time. I was right.

Even if it was to do with her past, I wanted her to see a good doctor who could help her get better. I was not in favour of her current doctor, Dr Bose, because Ayra had been seeing her for a few years and things had just worsened. They had gone from bad to worse, and only Ayra could not see that.

After she came back and sat in the taxi next to me, I realized that she had lost some more weight in the last few weeks. The dress was not as snug on her as it was when we had purchased it after we got married. 'We are going to a doctor,' I told her sternly, and she gave me a look that screamed a big 'NO!'

'But why?' I asked, worried for her.

'Because we are on our honeymoon and we can go and visit a doctor when we go back to India,' she answered, and shushed me. I still asked the Uber driver to take us to a medical centre; the doctor was off duty for the day, and the duty nurse prescribed some basic digestive remedies.

Even though I was angry at her for not taking good care of herself, I did not say much until we were back in our hotel room. I didn't want the Uber driver to see us fight.

'Why can we not see another doctor?' I asked her again when she finally joined me back in the bed. She looked tired and worn out. Her hair were tied back and made her look like a schoolgirl who was being reprimanded on a day when she wanted to just sit at the last bench and sleep.

'Can we talk about this tomorrow, please?' She put her arms around me, and I couldn't help but notice how they had become skinnier. Why did I not notice this before today? I was amazed at my own clumsiness.

'No,' I snarled and realized that I should not have reacted so with her. She was unwell and needed rest. 'Okay,' I added quickly. 'But we need to close this tomorrow,' I told her in a stern voice and felt her smile against my chest. I held her close to me as my life depended upon her. It did; she had changed me so much and for the better and I didn't want anything to happen to her. She believed that what she had was a small problem while I believed that her doctor was her problem.

It was finally decided that Ayra would take a second opinion after my family intervened and told the stubborn girl that seeking medical help was okay when needed and it didn't come across as a sign of weakness. My mother gave her many examples where small problems had troubled people for a really long time just because they had been misdiagnosed. Finally, Ayra had no other option but to give in.

My parents called us once a day, every day, mostly during evenings as we were five and a half hours ahead of them. They had both been to Australia more than a few times and were the ones who suggested that we visit all the beaches and go to Manjit's whenever we craved good Indian food. Mummy missed me more while Ayra had become Papa's pet from the beginning. He was fond of her positivity as well as her attitude. He had more than once mentioned that she was the reason why I had gotten more sincere and responsible in a short period of time. 'Pfff' was my reaction to his statement, but I did know that he was right. And I was very happy and grateful that Ayra had chosen to be with me despite all my flaws.

Her parents, on the other hand, never called us. They did text Ayra once in a while to know if we were all doing well. This is what she usually told me even though she had never shown or shared those texts with me. I didn't expect anything from them and had kind of made peace with it. Her sister, Somya, did call her once a week as she lived in America and the sisters had a lengthy heart to heart chat.

The next day, we both woke up late and I called in for some breakfast in bed. It was decided that we would spend our day in and around the city as it was our last day in Sydney and we were to head back to Delhi. Ayra had a college friend named Suhani, who was in Sydney. She had been away visiting her family in India and was back in the city that same day. Upon knowing that we were to leave the next day itself, she invited us to come and meet her. They lived in a place called Parramatta, which was some twenty-five minutes away from our hotel. As she was feeling better that morning and really wanted to meet her old friend, I could not say no to Ayra's request. It was decided that we were to meet for lunch at around one in Parramatta.

Upon arrival at her home, I realized that Suhani was married to an Australian bloke named Brian. He surprised the two of us with his barbecue plans, and so, we followed our hosts. After a quick round of non-alcoholic drinks, the four of us went to a park near their home. I was amazed to see that more than three barbecue stations were available to be used at the park. Brian and I hit it off very well, and I helped him as much as I could with the barbecue. The girls chatted happily while sitting under the shade, waiting for their food to be served. I felt relaxed to see Ayra in the company of her friend as she talked animatedly. All my worries around her health vanished as I believed that she would be better in no time as soon as we visited a good doctor.

After lunch, we bid Brian and Suhani goodbye and took an Uber to go back to our hotel. The cab broke down midway, and we decided against taking another taxi for the rest of our journey. Instead, we went out on foot. It was a sunny day, and we needed hats. So, we made a quick halt to shop for hats at a nearby market. What was to be a quick stop extended to two hours and we indulged in a much-needed retail therapy. With more than a few items in our shopping bag, which mostly included gifts for people back home, we headed back to the hotel. It was a fun walk, which had tired us out more than we had anticipated. There was nothing planned for the day, so we took a long afternoon nap, and then in the evening, we were out at the harbour bridge, enjoying ferry rides, walks, and coffee.

The next day, we bid goodbye to Australia with a heart full of memories and bags full of gifts for people in India who had been missing us. Apart from the gifts for our families, we also had protein shakes and vitamin supplements, which my cousins had requested me to get from Australia. We reached back home on Sunday, and the very next day, I dragged Ayra, against her wishes, to our family consultant at Max Hospital. Mummy wanted to come along as well, but I knew that Ayra was very sensitive about her health. All her present health issues were related to her mental health, and I wanted her to be at ease when talking to the doctor. So, I told Mummy to stay at home, and Ayra and I went to the hospital to meet Dr Sharma.

Even though Dr Sharma is a physician, I wanted his opinion on her condition before we were referred to someone else. Our family treated him like family; he had even attended our reception a few days ago.

A Week Later.

We had seen Dr Sharma at his office already. He is an amiable chubby man who likes to talk about all the things one can possibly think of under the sun. The day he met Ayra and me for the first time regarding her health, he cracked jokes about his own health and made her feel at home. That was the first thing that he did for everyone, I guess. It was vital for him that his patients felt at ease while he asked them the uneasy questions. We had booked an appointment with him early in the morning, which lasted for more than an hour. After the session, he asked us to sit outside for a while and then we were called in again. Very professionally, in front of me, Dr Sharma asked Ayra if she was okay with me being in the same room when another doctor, Dr Neeta Mehra, who is a psychologist, joined him and Ayra in the room. I had no issues walking out of the room as the patient's comfort is the most important thing, but Ayra chose to meet Dr Mehra in front of me. She did, however, ask Dr Sharma a few questions about Dr Mehra and explained to him her relation with her present psychologist.

Soon, Dr Neeta Mehra joined us, and Dr Sharma introduced us to her. She was a middle-aged woman with a motherly vibe. Her smile was reassuring, and she looked like she had a lot of experience in her field. She probed Ayra with easy questions that soon led to the harder ones. After about fifteen minutes, she took Ayra away with her as she wanted to ask her some more questions in private. I was left in the company of Dr Sharma, who had patients waiting for him. As expected, I was soon waiting outside Dr Mehra's office for what felt like ages for Ayra to appear. Both Mummy and Papa had called a few times to check if they were needed. I had to tell them to be wherever they were because we would be back soon. 'There is no point coming over, Mummy. By the time you get ready and start your journey to the hospital, we shall be back home,' I tried to reassure my mother, but failed at the attempt, miserably.

'Okay,' she sounded unsure of what I had said and unwillingly disconnected the call. They were making me more nervous than the doctors. Anyhow, after what felt like an hour, Ayra came out looking for me. Dr Mehra wanted to talk to me. It turned out that I was not alone. Dr Mehra was not very convinced with Ayra's favourite doctor's diagnosis as well. When I went inside her cabin to meet her, she suggested that we consult a few other doctors to figure out the root cause of her health issues, as her symptoms did not just point towards her mental health. She did not discuss Ayra's mental health with me, but she did explain to me why she thought we needed further investigation. Honestly, I never anticipated how vast the science is, and even though I did not really have any prejudices in my mind related to mental health, talking to her widened my horizons and made me understand things better. She believed that Ayra's health might have initially declined because of her diagnosed depression, but what she was suffering at the moment was not just related to her mind and thoughts; her body was showing signs of some physical distress that needed to be addressed. 'Her problem could be as small as an internal swelling, but it is physical and not just psychological. I would want you guys to meet a few doctors as soon as you can, so that they can begin with their tests,' she suggested, and I could not have agreed with her more.

Ayra looked nervous, maybe even a little scared. I held her hand as soon as we stepped out of Dr Sharma's cabin, to assure her. Her eyes were watery, and she leaned onto me for support. 'All will be well, trust me,' I said to her, but no words could help.

It would be wrong to say that I was not worried for her then. I was worried for her as much as she was worried for herself, if not more. But I believed it to be something minor that could be treated in no time. She was losing weight because she was throwing up, and as soon as the doctors could fix the reason why she kept throwing up, it would all be fixed. This was my firm belief. The mind makes you look at only the positive side when it comes to your loved ones. I was told to come back with Ayra the next day to the same place. Dr Mehra's receptionist had arranged the next couple of medical appointments for us.

Before leaving the hospital, I again went back in to meet Dr Sharma. He was busy with a patient of his, and we had to wait for some time before he called us in. His face had the same smile on it, and yet, I could sense that something had changed. I asked him if he had heard from Dr Mehra, and if at all, it was worth going further with the investigation. As expected, he said it was essential that we visited Dr Mehra and go forward with what she had suggested. He assured us just like Dr Mehra had. 'She will be well in no time. She is so young and looks perfectly fine, too. There was no reason to worry about it. A young body can beat almost every health problem and come out as a winner,' he told me, patting my back, perhaps sensing that I needed some strength, too, to be able to stand with her while she makes the journey.

Ayra was more upset after her appointments that she was before. We had our first loud fight as a married couple in the car that evening as we returned home. 'Why are we doing this, Sahil? I do not look very unwell, even as per the doctor! I do not like it when they suck so much blood out of me just for conducting millions of tests. I am okay. You know that I am not sick, right?'

I felt bad for putting her through all this trouble. Dr Sharma did say that she looked alright, but then he also suggested that we do as per the suggestions of Dr Mehra. I was torn between the two options, and it was getting difficult to choose with every passing minute. Her questions had put me in a spot. I believed that everything was okay, and I also knew that there was no harm in getting a few tests done for our peace of mind.

'What is the harm if we can eliminate the possibilities of anything being wrong? I am sure that they will be doing some generic tests to eliminate the possibility of digestive issues like stones and all. You will not have to shed gallons of blood, I give you my word, and then I will be stress-free. Please go through this for me, please,' I begged and took my eyes off the road while the car stood still at a red light near the hospital. Her face had puffed up in anger. I had never seen her that angry. To lighten her mood, I connected the music system in the car to my phone and played her favourite song, 'Pyaar Deewana Hota Hai'. She loved retro Hindi numbers, and they were an instant mood fixer for her, but that day, the trick did not work either.

She picked up my phone and paused the song. I didn't dare to look at her. After some silence, she said, 'What shall we tell Mummy and Papa?' She was referring to my parents, of course, as we hardly spoke about her parents after marriage.

'Nothing! We do not need to tell them or anyone else anything.' I placed my hand on her freezing palm. She was nervous as well as anxious then, and I understood her concern; she was worried. My parents, however, are the most positive people on the planet who loved her dearly; all they ever wanted for us was happiness and health. But if I tried to explain that to her, the conversation might have steered in the wrong direction, so I decided to drop the topic instead. Moreover, I had planned a surprise back home for her, and I knew that all her worries and troubles were to vanish the moment I showed her what the surprise was.

'Really? And how would you explain tomorrow's hospital visit to Papa, who is expecting to see you at the office with him,' she reasoned. I had been working through the details of a back-up plan in my head already. Ayra wanted to rejoin her office, and I had suggested that she should first finish her children's book. She was nearly done, and only some last-minute work was left, so that it was ready to be pitched for publication. I intended to lie to my parents, and her book had to be our shield. We would tell them that she and I had to meet some agents to get her a publishing deal. I knew that neither of them would mind it.

As soon as we reached home, Mummy forced us to sit at the dining table for lunch. It was two in the afternoon, and despite all the stress, I was starving. Mummy had prepared a lavish meal for the two us that afternoon. Papa was back for lunch as well. It was a rare occasion, as Mummy sent Papa's lunch to his office every day. It was only for Ayra that Papa had broken his habit and was eating his afternoon meal with us. Naturally, after lunch, there were questions around the hospital visits and our meeting with Dr Sharma.

'What is he suggesting now? Did you guys meet any specialists?' Papa asked, slicing his gulab jamun into two pieces with a spoon.

'He says all looks good, Papa. There is no need to meet anyone else as such, as of now,' I lied boldly in front of my parents and looked at Ayra. Her gaze was fixed at the sweet dish in her hand. She had barely eaten anything for lunch and going by the looks of it, I was sure that her sweet was going to be wasted as well.

Thankfully, Papa didn't stretch the topic any further. Mummy, however, made an observation around Ayra losing weight. 'She has lost so much in the last one month itself,' she said, genuinely concerned. She partly blamed me for not keeping her happy by taking her out on dates, parties, outings and for movies, like a newly married man should. I took the blame and promised my parents to take better care of her to keep her happier. The discussion was interrupted when the servant came in to collect the dishes from the room and informed Papa that someone had come to meet him. Ayra and Mummy decided to watch some TV, and I sneaked out to check how my wedding present (which was a surprise) was shaping up.

After dinner, Ayra and Mummy watched their TV shows, and I quietly slipped into Papa's room to let him know that I would not be going to the office the next day. I am sure that I looked terribly upset and very tensed that evening. Papa noticed it as soon as he lifted his eyes to meet mine when I knocked at the door of his home office. He had his reading glasses on, and I noticed that he had a big pile of documents in front of him as well. His work was expanding; we had plans to open a software testing centre to cater to a few potential clients in America. I was working on it with Papa before the wedding and was to take over my responsibilities again as soon as we were back. 'How far are we with the investors?' I asked him, stepping inside and scanning the documents. The investment was a challenge for Papa in the USA as we had lesser contacts there. I was supposed to help him sort that out, but there I was, approaching him to ask for a few more days off, just like in college when I always asked my professors for extra days for the projects and assignments. But this was unlike anything at college; I was not asking for a few days off to hang out with my friends or to waste time doing nothing. I was going to ask for a few days to be with my wife who needed my support.

I knew that, but I was scared that Papa wouldn't understand the gravity of the issue, and I had promised Ayra that I would not be explaining anything to avoid scaring them. But I had to tell him that I couldn't join the office just yet. I had planned to work on the project from home after the hospital visits. 'America and India have a time gap of twelve hours. I have to sacrifice on my sleep, but yes, I can do that,' I made an instant resolve and wondered how much I had changed. I was now thinking responsibly even when I knew that I could have escaped work without much questioning from my boss, who is also my father. But I wanted to do the right thing.

'It will happen, we shall make it happen,' Papa responded a bit absentmindedly and I agreed with him. He and I would get the investment sorted. 'I was thinking that I should work during the American working hours, Papa. I can work from home for a few days until everything falls in place,' I proposed hopefully and Papa saw sense in it as well.

'That makes more sense actually. What all would you need?' he asked me, finally raising his eyes off the documents.

'I will get all that arranged, you do not worry about it,' I assured him, and it was all sorted. No matter how tensed I was, the presence of my parents always relaxed me. Papa and I spoke for some time about the project and finalized a few things, which were pending at my end. I itched to talk to him about Ayra; he knew me so much better than anyone else did, and I really needed my father's advice, but his peace of mind was more important. Even though I needed someone to listen to me, I wanted someone close to me—someone, other than a doctor, someone who had known me forever to tell me that all was going to be okay. Because I was going to be missing from home the next morning and I knew that the topic was bound to be raised at the dinner table, I decided to tell Papa a bit of it so that our absence was expected the next day.

'There is a lump in Ayra's neck. The doctor thinks it could just be inflamed nodules or something else. They have asked us to visit them tomorrow again,' I told him not looking at him in the eye. I was breaking the trust of my wife; I was breaking the trust of a patient. Legally, I had no right to discuss her health with anyone, but there I was, venting it all out as I needed to be assured that the doctors would do as many tests as they could to eliminate all possibilities.

I wanted Papa to tell me that it was all going to be alright, and he did so, but he also surprised me by telling me that Dr Sharma had already told him a bit of what I was telling him. 'He was worried that the two of you might try and keep it all a secret. You might need some help; she might need help. It is best to tell us what is happening, so that we can be there to support you.' Papa was just as I wanted him to be, helpful and supportive.

Many people that I have met have told me that I have the most amazing parents in the world. There's no way that so many people can be wrong—I am indeed blessed to have the best parents, who have loved and supported me all my life. They have always known what my needs of the hour were and have been there for me no matter what. That evening, all I wanted was to unburden my worries. I was worried about Ayra, and I couldn't tell her. So, when Papa hugged me, he allowed me to unburden a troubled mind, and I instantly felt at ease. 'It was all going to be okay,' my heart told me, but the mind had too many questions.

If all was okay and these were only precautionary tests, then why did Dr Sharma call Papa? She looks healthy, then why are they doing these tests? What can a node in the throat mean? Her doctor had asked me to recall if at all, her voice had changed in the recent past—it had. It had gone coarse. Did this mean something? I had intended to do some research on my own, but being surrounded by family all the time had not given me any chance to do so.

'It could be something as small as an abnormal thyroid function, which is easily fixable,' Papa said, and I agreed. It was indeed going to be easily treatable. It had to be.

I made Papa promise me that he would act normal in Ayra's presence. 'She worries more than I do Papa, and she overthinks, too, just like Mummy does,' I told him jokingly, meaning every single word though. Papa understood my concern for her. She looked very worked up lately, and he promised me not to say a word or act unnaturally. We decided that Mummy need not know as she was the number one worrier in the household. With many questions, which could only be answered with time, I bid Papa goodnight. When I stepped out of their room, Mummy and Ayra were ready for bed as well.

CHAPTER 13

The Surprise.

After our marriage, Ayra and I were to share a bedroom on the second floor. Before going to Sydney, Ayra and I were allotted a temporary space on the first floor as there was some more work to be done on the new floor. Construction work was in full swing about the time we were to be married, and was halted for a few days due to the ceremonies. Finally, on that evening, it was finished, and my wife and I were to, for the very first time, sleep on our floor in 'our bedroom'.

The floor seemed like a well-designed, independent house with a fully-functional kitchen that we intended never to use. Ayra's love for the stars was so strong that I knew that my first present to her after we got married had to be something to do with it.

At around nine, we bid everyone goodnight and took the stairs to reach the second floor. Mummy had already arranged for all our belongings and clothes to be moved well ahead of time. Our bedroom was aesthetically decorated.

It had plain white walls with our pictures hung on one wall that was charcoal in colour. Ayra was happy and loved the new room. But that was not the gift. 'I have a surprise for you,' I told her, beaming with pride.

'Is this not a surprise?' she looked around and said, looking every bit happy that I had expected her to be.

'Noooo!' I replied and took out a blindfold from the pocket of my nightsuit. 'Turn around,' I told her, and she complied without any questions.

I tied the scarf as a blindfold loosely over her eyes and held her hand. Slowly, we walked out of the room, into the living space and then into the closed balcony.

'Here we are!' I whispered into her ears and took the scarf off her eyes.

She adjusted her vision and then her jaw dropped. It was indeed surreal; the designer had done a great job. I had asked for the balcony to be closed and for a rectangular-shaped glass ceiling to be constructed, under which there was a bed—a bed we could lie down on and look at the stars through our glass ceiling. As the balcony was closed and ours was the tallest house in the neighbourhood, there was no worry of a privacy breach either.

'This is so gorgeous!' she hugged and screamed.

'Do you like it?' I asked her, even though I knew that she loved it.

'I love it, and I love you!' she replied, and there, the most beautiful words in the world echoed in my ears.

When I had come up to check whether or not the work was done as per my satisfaction, I had set up some candles, and it was time to light them up and gaze at the stars.

Little did I know that this was going to be one of the best memories we would create together. The memories from the time we lay together—talking as we looked at the stars while lying on the bed—are so close to my heart that I do not wish to share them with anyone. They are so personal that I would not include those conversations in the book.

That night, no matter how much I tried to sleep, I could not sleep a wink. I got up many times just to see her sleeping next to me. Her breathing gave me the calmness that I needed. I saw her move a little every time she inhaled. The slow rise and fall of her breathing was a sight that gave me happiness. I touched her forehead, and she moved a little, murmuring my name in her sleep. She looked serene, and I felt at ease, just enough to lie back on the bed with her.

It was the first of many nights to come when we were sleeping under the stars. She loved it, and I loved everything that she loved. That night, I looked back at life and realized how soon things can change. There was a time, not very long ago, when I used to be worried about things like the future and my friends and even my college, but that night, all I wanted was her health and happiness. Priorities change in no time and make us different from what we were the day before. This is probably what is called 'growth in life'. This is what matters at the end of the day, and not the money or the status that most people run after.

Taking my eyes off the stars in the sky, I looked at her once again. She was lying in the cosy bed with me, wrapped up in a comforter, dreaming about something, looking happy and breathing softly. She was mine, and I was hers forever. I kissed her forehead one last time before checking the time. It was five in the morning; we had to be present at Dr Mehra's office sharp at nine-thirty. I held her tight and closed my eyes; there was no sleep in them, but my body needed some rest.

The Next Day

I woke up with the beautiful smell of her hair and her perfume. I rubbed my eyes to look around. She was not in bed anymore. I looked at my alarm clock; it was seven in the morning. I had set up an alarm for six-thirty, so I wondered how I managed to sleep through it. I checked the clock to find that the alarm was switched off. Ayra must have switched it off when she got up. I walked into the living room, looking for her and heard her humming. The sound was coming from our bedroom. I peeped in to find her drying her hair with a towel as she hummed an old Hindi song. I could not figure out which one, but it was a song that I had heard recently.

'Did you turn off the alarm, Mrs Malhotra?' I knew my question would startle her, but I did not realize the extent of it. She screamed out of her skin and looked at me as if I was a ghost.

'You scared me!' she pointed out and widened her eyes.

'That was the exact expression that I was aiming for,' I replied and winked at her to make her smile, but she ignored me and resumed her activities.

'We have to leave in another hour, so I thought that you could use some extra sleep,' she said after a while. 'You had been tossing and turning all night in the bed. All okay, brat?' she asked me, looking at my reflection in the mirror. I had tried to be as slow and low as I could have managed last night and yet she knew that I had difficulty sleeping.

'I was looking at you. You looked pretty last night,' I told her only half the truth.

'Haha,' she mocked a laugh and turned around. 'Very funny! Tell me, are you worried about today?' She knew the answer and was aware that what I had told her was only half the truth.

'No, you are healthy as a horse, and the doctors have just called you to figure out how. I know that you are healthy, it is all good,' my voice went low towards the end, and I knew it was time I went into the washroom to take a shower. I was probably just stressing over nothing and didn't want to scare her more.

'Hey! Try and come out soon as I want to go to a temple before we go to the hospital today,' she said softly, knocking on the bathroom door and I did as requested. I took only twenty minutes to join her at the breakfast table on the ground floor. All four of us had breakfast together, discussing politics and food. Mummy was in a good mood that morning as her daughter-in-law had managed to convince her son to go to the temple early in the morning. My mother goes to the ISKCON temple every morning at five and had asked me to drop or pick her up all her life. I had never done that because getting up early to go to the temple was never my thing, well, until that day at least.

Ayra and I went back upstairs to collect our things when she said that she would want to go to the temple whenever we have to go to the hospital for check-ups and tests. I took a while to comprehend what exactly she meant by that. I felt my heart thump as if I was about to be hit by a train.

'Why? Baby, it is just a routine check-up,' I leapt towards her and nervously held her. Her hair smelled nice, and I inhaled deeply. It was her shampoo, which was fruity. She looked lovely like a flower, fresh and bright. How could she even think of more tests? Why do women love to think so much?

'I know.' She gave me a kind of reassuring look and wriggled a little under my arms. I hugged her tighter. Did she know something that I did not? I had to ask her.

'What is it, tell me, please?' I held my breath for her answer. She did not lie to me, she never did. She told me that she had Googled all her symptoms—the ones that the doctors had questioned her about—and Google hinted at cancer.

'Cancer? Are you serious? Google is no doctor, and trust me, even if you Google the symptoms of the flu randomly, it will somehow lead to cancer. If you do not trust me, then go ahead and try it. Come on, try it!' I laughed at the end and heard her chuckle in my embrace. Even though I had made her smile, I was worried. *Cancer*? The word was scary enough. I prayed to god that it was anything but that. I had lost my grandmother to cancer, and it was the most painful thing.

We went to a nearby temple before heading towards the hospital. As it was a busy day, we just got seconds before the idols to pray. I looked at her; with her head bowed and her hands folded in prayer, she looked so calm. I prayed for her good health as that was the most important thing for us at that moment, and moments later, we were out on the road. Papa had insisted that we take the driver with us that day when we were stepping out of the house. Mummy gave us dahi and sugar for good luck as she was still under the impression that we were going to meet some literary agents.

Ayra was supposed to go to the hospital with an empty stomach that day, so she lied that she was fasting to skip eating. Mummy was easily convinced; she knew that girls were usually fasting for something or the other—her mother-in-law was the same. Finally, my parents bid us good luck and we moved along.

It was a long day for us. We met a lot of new doctors. Several blood tests were done, and Ayra went through a CT scan. Dr Mehra wanted to know how she was feeling that morning and decided to drop in and have a long chat with her, alone. Even though she was being looked after, I was not happy being there. *We shouldn't be here.* A panel of doctors was being consulted, and one after the other, someone or the other was there to see, talk to or test her. We were asked if we were comfortable getting a bed in the hospital.

Ayra, who was totally against the idea of coming to this hospital initially, suddenly started giving in to all demands of the doctors. This was the point when I knew that she knew something more than the rest of us, and by the 'rest of us', I mean my family and me. The doctors didn't tell me a thing until it was confirmed, as they worried that I would panic. When they wheeled her into the room, I lost it. 'You cannot do this, Ayra. We were not even supposed to come to this place. Why are they making you stay? Tell me at least that!' I started sobbing, sitting by her knees like a child whose mother was leaving him at the kindergarten to fend for himself.

'I do not feel very strong right now. The doctors think some rest will do me good. Can you please let Mummy and Papa know that I am not well?' At that moment, she gave me her permission to tell my parents about our whereabouts, and within hours, they were at her bedside. Mummy being Mummy was worried sick while Papa spoke to the doctors. I was still not considered to be a part of the information group, and this irked me more than anything else.

That night, I stayed with her in the hospital, and the next day, another test—a 'Fine Needle Aspiration Biopsy' was done. This was supposedly the last and the most painful test for her. With a bandage on her throat and some painkillers, Ayra was sent home with us. A few hours later, her reports came in, and we got a call from the hospital to bring her in as soon as we could. I told Papa and asked him if he too, like me, thought that we were rushing into things. 'We should take a second opinion, Papa,' I told him sternly, but he had left the decision of whether or not a second opinion was needed to Ayra. She wanted to go back to the hospital as advised by the doctors. She decided on her own that I was to be at home with Mummy and take care of Papa's work while Papa was to accompany her to the hospital.

'Why?' I asked her, looking as surprised as I was. 'Because you are a brat, and it is time to take up some responsibilities,' was her reply. She stuck her tongue out, and both of them disappeared in the car.

A while later, when Papa finally answered my calls from the hospital, I wanted to know how she was, and when they were coming back.

'What happened?' I asked Papa, 'What do the reports say?'

Papa took a while to answer. He began by saying that in today's day and age, everything is curable, and one should never take their faith off God as well as science. Suddenly, I felt as if I was the patient. I was being treated with so much calmness and care that I had started feeling frustrated about the whole process.

'I am coming there,' I told him and disconnected the call. I called Nishant, my cousin, to come over to my house and be with Mummy while I went to the hospital to see for myself how my wife was. When I reached there, she was resting in her room, and the nurse told me not to disturb her. I caught hold of Papa and demanded that it was time for him to spill the beans.

'Not here,' he told me and we walked away from Ayra's room. We stepped into the hospital cafeteria, where a few staff members were having tea. Papa made me sit at a table and took the chair next to mine. He was calm, but I knew that something was wrong—utterly and disappointingly wrong.

'You will have to calm yourself down; you are not the patient here, she is.' His opening statement was true, to say the least, and I did acknowledge that I was a little too rash and brash.

'I am sorry, but no one is telling me anything!' I protested, shrugging my shoulders and looking down at my sweaty hands. 'The suspense is killing me.'

'I am here to tell you, am I not?' Papa said and added, 'Ayra has what is known as "medullary thyroid cancer" in medical terms. Now before you panic, do know that this type of cancer is mostly treatable and she is very young to die from it.' He talked to me calmly, but a storm had already erupted in my mind.

'Cancer? Cancer!' I said and took my head in my hands. 'Does she know?' This was the first thing that came to me—was she aware all along?

'Yes, she knows now, but she was not aware of it until the tests were done. She did know about the possibility when she went through the tests as she was told about the same by the doctors. She did her research too and had a fair idea. She took the news bravely and spoke about her options and treatment, etc., all on her own, in my presence. She is a brave girl, Sahil; she will get out of it. *You* have to be strong. We need to help her and support her as much as we can so that her recovery happens as soon as it can and she comes out stronger . . .'

I lost my father there. I didn't know how to meet her, how to look her in the eye, or what to tell her anymore. Papa did say that her cancer was treatable, and yes, she was young, so her chances of beating it were higher, but it was still cancer. She had been through so much in her life, and now when her life had finally started to look bright, this hit her. It was so unfair! But then, I knew what a fighter I was married to. Our love gave me a lot of strength and Papa, and I went back to talk to the doctors. Ayra was taken into immediate care, and her treatment was to begin soon.

CHAPTER 14

The next many days of mine were spent in and out of the hospital. My parents were by my side, and so were my cousins. Bhanu, as well, had come over to meet Ayra, three days after she was first admitted into the cancer ward. His visits continued, and Pathak accompanied him on several occasions. Many of Ayra's office colleagues dropped by as well and kept her company on days when she needed people by her side. Not after very long, it was established that her cancer had very quietly spread around her thyroid gland. Small nodes had formed, and thus, surgery was not possible at that time to remove them all. A surgery could help the cancer from spreading further, and she had to go through chemo first, to bring it under control. We were referred to a specialist surgeon in Noida, and without wasting much time, we did as we were told.

The day after we got the news of her disease, Ayra and I had called her parents to let them know of the diagnosis. Surprisingly, they didn't come to meet their ill daughter. They were busy with some renovations in their house, and it was not deemed safe to leave the household and come all the way to meet her. 'Do you want to meet them?' I asked her, knowing that she did. She didn't say anything, just stared blankly out of the window. Ayra had started doing this very often lately, and her sudden detachment from everyone worried me. So, the first time when she was out of the hospital, I took her to meet her parents, who looked happy to see her. They expressed their concerns around her health and also mentioned how an astrologer had long ago predicted that she might die young. I remained quiet all through the meeting; there was nothing much to talk about anyway.

I never met them again.

CHAPTER 15

July 2018

Life was running past us, and we were trying to figure out how to stop time. But time never stops for anyone or anything. No matter how much you clench your fist, grains of time fall through it, to never be found again. Without telling her, I had sent Ayra's book idea to many publishers, and more than a few were happy to take up the book.

While Ayra put on a brave face, what came as the biggest surprise was the way my mother handled everything. I had always thought of Mummy to be the one who would break down under pressure, but during those months, I realized why Papa referred to her as the 'kingmaker'. Mummy became the rock-solid foundation of our house. She became the mother that Ayra never had; she became her go-to person. Every dose of her medicine, every appointment with the doctor, every time there was a change in her schedule—Mummy knew it, and she was there for her. I saw their relationship evolve in no time. There were days when I stepped out of the house for an urgent meeting or to get updates from a publisher, but my mind was as peaceful as Ayra was with my Mummy, who took much better care of her than I did.

Her illness had not just impacted our house, but of many others, too. Bhanu and Pathak reconciled with their families in Delhi and soon moved back closer to home. Life is uncertain, and things happen when we do not even expect them to; wasting even a single minute in remorse, hatred or anger is not worth it as life is precious and so are relations. We are all humans, and humans make mistakes.

After moving back, Bhanu and Pathak started coming over to our home almost every evening, whenever Ayra was not in the hospital. We loved having dinner together as my mother's recipes and Bhanu's cooking skills were a deadly combo. Most evenings, especially when we had company, Ayra was the most cheerful. She had some limitations of speech, so I would sing and dance with Bhanu and Pathak for her after Papa and Mummy would retire for the night. Some days, we went on long drives, as walks were not an option in her state. Even though our bed under the stars was scarcely used, whenever we did lie on it, I recorded all our conversations. She didn't know about it, of course, but I needed her voice to be with me, for life. I need her words to inspire me for life. Some nights, after many painful sessions, Ayra insisted on staying up late and we lay there, intertwined with each other, gazing at the endless stars in the galaxy.

Doctors tried medicines and treatments one after the other, but nothing was making her better. Even though everyone had assumed that her body, being young, would respond to almost all types of modern treatment, it was not true. Her body was weak and tired from all the fighting against this deadly disease for the past many months. She was tired and said this every time we headed back to the hospital. 'Hey, brat! I do not like being in bed anymore. Can we do something fun instead of going back?' she said every time I packed her green hospital bag. I had no other option but to lovingly caress her cheeks until she knew that we had to go no matter what and then I used to cry some silent tears in the washroom, away from her.

By early July 2018, a new method of treatment was tested on her, and her condition began to improve. Even though she lost weight day after day, her zeal to live was as strong as it had always been and her cancer appeared to be in control. It was a happy phase in our life after what felt like forever, and that was the same time when her book was nearly on the verge of being published as well. I finally told her that her dream was going to come true, but Ayra being herself, forced me to postpone the release.

'Can you please tell me why?' I asked her, stroking her hair, and pretending to be mad. I had stopped being mad at her or at anyone for that matter. Life is too short to be mad; it is so unpredictable that every waking moment should be spent enjoying life, enjoying health and enjoying the company of our loved ones.

'I will publish the book only after you at least finish writing yours.' She gave me a task, and I knew that she wanted me to write at least one book in her lifetime. This was also the time when she started leaving me these small handwritten notes. Why? Because, she didn't want to go away one day, with even a single thought or emotion lying in her head unsaid, unwritten, or unheard. We said 'I love you' to each other countless times a day because no matter how many times we did say the words to each other, it was still not enough to last a lifetime—our future could not be predicted. It could have been as long as fifty years of togetherness or as short as fifty minutes. Every moment was to be lived and loved.

I woke up every morning with the hope of a miracle. We had tried more than a few revolutionary methods of care and treatment in the past two months, and more than once, we had been given hope of recovery. Despite Ayra's age, her body seemed to be rejecting all medication after the initial few days. It was as if it had resolved that it would not take any help. By mid-July, her weight loss was under control, and she looked visibly happy as well as bright. She insisted on meeting new people every day, so after hospital visits, we would go to nursing homes, orphanages and parks. She would chat with the old and play with the kids. I carried my camera and diary everywhere, so that I missed no moment with her. 'Everything has to go in the book,' I had resolved, but now, when I am writing it, I did not want to share most of the details of her last days. I want those memories all for myself.

The doctors were happy with her progress in the last few weeks, and in my previous meeting, her doctor had assured me that she still had a lot of time. After all, she is responding so well, and she looks so happy, too. 'And you never know what can happen tomorrow; maybe she will be cured on her own,' my mother, who was always very positive about Ayra's health, kept telling me every day. Papa had stopped going to the office altogether, and all work was being managed from home. As a family, we spent the majority of our time together on the ground floor. Our bedroom had moved to the ground floor as well, owing to Ayra's condition, which meant we spent fewer nights under the stars and more days with our loved ones.

During evenings, we would lie on the couch and watch cartoons, or *The Big Bang Theory*, night after night.

Bhanu and Pathak had finally managed to buy a new house in the city. Not many people were willing to sell the property as they were a same-sex couple, and their struggle made us question so many things, which are wrong in our society. Anyhow, they intended to do a small get-together for house-warming and kept rescheduling it week after week for they wanted both Ayra and me to be present. On the fifth of August, the day when we completed nine months of our marriage, Ayra's doctors told me that she was improving well and a new dose of drugs had been introduced, which would make her extra sleepy and lethargic. Around this time, she was on a liquid diet and spoke very less. With her body still weak, we had stopped going out, so her attending Bhanu and Pathak's house-warming was not possible. They understood that, too. I wanted to skip the party as well, because Ayra was the one that I wanted to be with, but she insisted that I go. That evening, she opened her eyes and checked the time; it was time for me to go to the house-warming party without her and I didn't want to go. She smiled weakly at me and closed her eyes to go back into her slumber. Looking at her lying in bed, so pale and tired, broke my heart into a million pieces.

Mummy and Papa had left for Jammu to pray for her health at the Vaishno Devi temple.

I called Bhanu to let him know that we would not be able to make it to their house-warming as I did not want to leave her all alone with just a nurse and servant in the house. Bhanu was more than understanding. 'I will cancel it,' he said to me instead, when I explained my situation to him.

'No, no!' I protested, 'Do not do such a thing. I am sure Ayra wouldn't want that. She would have loved to be a part of your happiness, and now when she can't, I speak on her behalf to tell you that you should host the most amazing and rocking party for your new home.' I almost choked on my tears by the end of the sentence, and Bhanu went quiet for a while to give me some time and space to recover.

Somewhere, I knew that she was in a lot of pain and that drifting away with the least amount of pain was the best for her. She had been in so much pain that a part of me wanted her to be free from it soon and be peaceful. But then again, there was this selfish part that wanted her to stay with me no matter what state she was in. I was nothing without her.

I took a washroom break and then went into the bedroom to see how she was. She was up again as her new nurse had arrived. Not very long ago, doctors had suggested we keep a medical professional in the house to monitor her condition, and Papa agreed. 'Nothing but the best for my daughter,' he said, controlling his emotions and I thanked him with all my heart. After her nurse checked her vitals and went into the kitchen to get some water for herself, Ayra pointed towards my bedside—there was a note on it. She wanted me to go to Bhanu and Pathak's party.

'Why?' I mouthed.

Ayra patted the space next to her on our bed, and I sat down there, holding her hand as if I was holding her for life as if she was my only chance of survival, which she was. She lifted her left hand and gently ran her fingers through my hair, bringing it down to touch my cheeks and then my lips. She placed her finger on my lips and said in a very low voice, 'Go, for me.' I could have never said no to her, and I never did.

5 September 2018

The doctors had finally decided to go ahead with her surgery, which meant that soon, Ayra was to be operated upon, and the cancer was going to be removed from her body. It was the most amazing piece of news which came to us in a very long time and that too on the day when we completed ten months of our married life.

I immediately called Mummy and Papa and told them what I had just heard. Ayra was still with the doctors, undergoing the last round of her chemo. As expected, my parents were over the moon. I had been following a custom every month on the date we got married, and there was no reason not to continue with it that evening as well.

As per custom, I filled our bedroom with sunflowers, which were her favourite and played Jagjit Singh songs to wake her up from her afternoon nap. I opened the curtains, and warm sun-rays fell on her face. She opened her eyes and adjusted her vision; she had stopped wearing her glasses for the past few weeks as its weight hurt her nose. She looked tired but was happy. Feeling the delicate petals of yellow and red sunflowers which lay around her, she and I wondered how far we had come together and how it won't take very long for her to be perfectly healthy again. 'I would want you to cook for me as soon as you get permission to leave this bed,' I joked with her, and she smiled and nodded, while I showered her with tender kisses on her hands. 'So, when did you know that I was the one for you?' I asked her, wanting to make her talk about us.

'I knew that someday there would be a boy who would remember my favourite flowers. He might not have enough money to buy them, but he will know which ones are the ones he would buy when he has money. I knew that a boy would come into my life, who will learn my favourite song. He might never sing it for me but play it on his phone and then hum along softly. I knew that such a boy would come and earn my heart and soul, and then you came crashing into my life.' She touched my chest with her palms as if trying to feel my beating heart; the heart that was beating just for her. She spoke very less those days and to hear her speak so much was wonderful. Her nurse came in at that very moment, and I had to give them both their privacy as she bathed and changed Ayra.

I decided to call our friends, who had been with us through thick and thin to let them know. Her family had to be informed, too. So, I called her parents first, as calling friends would have taken longer as the conversations would have lasted for hours.

Her mother broke down; she cried and then told me that she would call me back after telling Ayra's father. I waited and waited, but there was no call back from her. When I called her back after a few hours, she told me that they were very happy with the development but won't be able to drop by as Ayra's elder sister was having a baby and both her parents had to be on a flight the next day to go to America and be with the expectant mother. I said nothing more. I thanked her for her wishes and disconnected the call. I was getting another call on my mobile from an unknown landline number in Delhi.

It was her doctor. He had some good news—a surgery was scheduled the coming week, and we had to travel to Mumbai where the best surgeon was to operate on Ayra. I informed Papa, and an air ambulance was arranged for the day we had to leave. It was all falling into place, and I couldn't have been more grateful or happier than I was. But I did have a task at hand—I had to tell Ayra that her parents were not going to be able to make it.

I needed Mummy's help. Mummy suggested that she would like to talk to Ayra's mother once before we told her anything. Mummy tried persuading them to come over as it would help build Ayra's morale, but her pleas fell on deaf ears. Finally, she and I told Ayra that her family was going to the USA, and they wanted to come over and meet her, but we asked them not to as she needed rest. It was a white lie, and Ayra knew it, but telling her the truth was more painful.

After Mummy left us alone again, I sat on the bed next to Ayra and told her all about the arrangements for her surgery in Mumbai. That was the moment when I had first noticed it—she looked different. I wondered if she looked the way she did because her painkillers were wearing off. 'Is everything okay, baby?' I asked her, rubbing her bird-like shoulders.

'Yes, everything is okay, but I would prefer if no one lies to me again,' she said, looking disappointed in me.

'I am sorry. I didn't want you to be sad over something that you and I have absolutely no control over,' I reasoned.

'You and I have no control over anything, brat! It is all controlled by our fates, destiny,' she said and adjusted herself on the bed. I helped her sit upright with the help of a few more pillows under her back.

'I do not like them,' I said, not looking into her eyes. It was a fact; I didn't like her adoptive parents because they had not taken up any responsibility.

'Learn to love people for what they have done and not hate them for what they haven't. They gave me a place to stay when they could have easily thrown me out. They made me study in good schools even though I was not their own. They took care of my needs when I couldn't. They treated me like a human, and that is what is most important.' She never failed to amaze me. I had nothing more to say other than taking back my words, and I did just that.

That evening, she looked the happiest in quite some time, and I was convinced that she was not leaving us anymore. 'Miracles do happen,' I kept repeating in my head, again and again, looking at her. It was indeed a miracle that the new drug had worked on her and that her cancer would soon be out of her body. She was beating all odds. She was a fighter, my fighter.

We retired late at night after it was confirmed that we were all going to Mumbai in the next few days as Mummy and Papa wanted to come along too. I didn't protest against their decision. It was a relief to have my family there for us at that hour. That evening, she wanted to spend some time under the star-lit sky. With the help of her nurse, I moved Ayra to the second floor after both my parents had gone to bed. My wife and I lay for many more hours under the star-lit sky. I felt her warm breath on my cheeks, and that gave me assurance for the future.

Sometime at night around two when I woke up, I could not feel her breathing on me anymore. I checked and saw that she lay in the same position. I stumbled upon a few things and got up to switch on the lights. Her big brown eyes were open; she lay gazing at the sky. I called out her name but she didn't respond. Her mouth was slightly open, and I could see a lone tear at the corner of her right eye. I went closer to the bed and kept my hand on her heart; it was lying silently in her, not beating nor moving.

There, wrapped in my arms under the sky filled with millions of stars, she left the world and me.

She left to become one of the brightest stars in the sky.

27 September 2018

This would have been her first birthday as my wife. I had never pictured how exactly I wanted it to be. I had planned nothing, as if I was aware that she would not be around. I felt sad that my own pessimism was killing me; she did leave me before her birthday, so my gut was right. Or maybe, I had just manifested it all. They say that you get what you truly believe to be yours—did I truly and with all my heart want her to die? No, it can't be. I wanted her to be with me till the end of time; till eternity.

'This "manifesting thing into our lives" is all bullshit,' I muttered and then recalled that during her last few days, I did want her to die. Not because I loved her any less or because I wanted her to be out of my life as soon as possible, but because I loved her even more than I did when we got married. I loved her truly and deeply and couldn't bear her suffering. Maybe, I did ask god to take her away peacefully as she deserved better than all the pain that she was being put through. My Ayra was and is an inspiration to me, she believed in me more than anyone else did; she made me a better version of my own self every day that she was with me; she believed that I could write this book and she believed that I could be whatever I wanted to be.

Suddenly, the doorbell rang and I paused my typing. It was midnight; the date had changed from twenty-four to twenty-five on all electronic devices near me. The world was to wake up in a few hours to begin their lives like nothing had happened, while I was sitting there getting drenched in the rain of her memories. I wondered who was at the door. We never had any visitors in the house past eight. I was in the same room where she left me. I come and sit there all night, every night. I did not want even her smell to escape the place, so I let no one, not even the servants, to enter it. I wanted to be with whatever I had of her for as long as possible.

When the bell rang again, I was fully convinced that it was not my tiredness playing games with me—someone was indeed at the door. The tired servants must've slept, and there was no need to wake them up at that hour. So, I got up, switched on the lights of the living area and peeped outside through the peephole. I saw a man dressed in red clothes standing at the door holding a bouquet of flowers and a few other things. I figured that he must have lost his way and opened the door to direct him. I am aware that people do plan surprises for their loved ones at midnight for birthdays and probably he was there was the same. 'Ayra would have done something like this for me. She was so good at planning surprises,' I could not help thinking. But it was not my birthday, it was hers.

'Sahil Malhotra?' he asked, surprising me.

'Yes,' I adjusted my glasses and looked at the packets in his hand—two boxes of what appeared to be chocolates and something else, some flowers and a note.

'This is for you, sir,' the lanky young fellow handed over all things to me and disappeared swiftly, or maybe he took his time, but when I failed to utter anything to him, he left disappointed because no tip was offered. I can only guess.

'Who could have sent these?' I didn't care much, but still, I looked at the box of chocolates—they were Ferrero Rochers, my favourite. The bouquet was a mix of sunflowers and roses and the last box on which the note was stuck was light as if it had nothing.

Confused and angry at the person who hardly cared about hurting my feelings at this time, I went back in and dumped all the things on the couch. 'I have to get back to writing,' I muttered to myself. I knew that I would not be able to concentrate till the time I opened the note and found out who thought of this vile prank. So, I dragged myself back into the living room and ripped open the envelope containing a printed note.

To Me,

Happy Birthday!

I knew that you would forget. Anyhow, as I cannot eat anything just yet, the chocolates are for you and the flowers are mine, even the roses. The gift is 'ours'.
May we be together forever.

With Love.

I dropped down on the floor crying, with my cries echoing all through the room. I was alone, and yet, she was there for me, with me. After many moments, with trembling hands, I opened the box with the gift in it. There was a digital photo frame. I switched it on, and all our memories started flashing in front of my eyes on it. It contained pictures from our first date until our honeymoon. I sobbed more as the images changed one after the other. No matter what I had manifested in her life, she believed that she would be there on this day. She hoped that she would live for longer than she did. Why was she taken at such a young age? I cannot help but wonder. She had so much to offer, so much to give to the world and me.

'People who are too good for the world die and become stars'—her words came back to me and I spend the rest of my night lying down on our bed, holding the photo frame close to my chest, staring at the stars, looking for her.

EPILOGUE

Love does not necessarily mean living together for eternity. I loved her, and I still do, but we are not together; we cannot be, as life doesn't care for the plans that we make. Life has its own plans; life decides things for us. Life is harsh, cruel and unfair, but this is what it is. Some call it fate, others call it karma—she called it 'our time' in the play of life.

No matter how much I try to cling on to your memories, your smell, your imprints in my life, slowly things will fade away. Even in my dreams when I shall see you, your face will start to blur with time and so will the detailed memories of our time together. All that my mind will contain are the important bits and pieces of these moments. Our mind is smarter than we think; it knows that after a loss, one shall perish if they live in the past forever, so it starts to replace the old memories with new ones and soon, one cannot revisit the same memories which one thought was just a thought away. The mind works on maintaining sanity by losing the past; my mind shall work on keeping my sanity by losing you.

But I do know that I will always remember our love, and our time together. There will always be pictures to refer to. It is the smell, your presence that I still feel around me, the laughter that still echoes in my mind, and the memory of your touch that I am still clinging on to that will disappear. Everyone that I meet tells me how much they miss you and how they would want you to come back, but I think that they are all wrong. They think that they miss you, but they do not for their lives are moving ahead—I am the only one who is still trapped in time where you left me. They wish that you would come back, but they had not seen you in pain during the last few days, they had not seen you suffer so much that even I prayed to god for your suffering to end, even if it meant that I would lose you forever. They do not realize how difficult it would be if at all, their wishes come true.

I know you are in a happy place now. I know you are watching me from up there. I gaze up every night trying to figure out which one of the bright stars you are, but you never give me a hint.

Something I Never Told You

When in love, you tend to take each other for granted, and sometimes, that can cost you a lifetime of togetherness . . .

Ronnie knew that his first crush was way out of his league, and yet he pursued and wooed Adira. Shyly and from a distance in the beginning, and more persuasively later. He couldn't believe it when the beautiful Adira actually began to reciprocate, falling in love with him for his simplicity and honesty.

Slowly, as they get close and comfortable with each other, life takes on another hue. From truly magical, it becomes routine. There are fights and then making-up sessions, a clash of egos and doubts.

Things begin to change for the worst.

It is too late.

Ronnie and Adira will probably never find their forever after . . .